BOGUS LOVER

BOGUS LOVER

HY SILVER

CUTTING EDGE

ISBN-13: 978-1-957868-74-5

Published by
Cutting Edge Books
PO Box 8212
Calabasas, CA 91372
www.cuttingedgebooks.com

INTRODUCTION

HY SILVER: THE PETALUMA CHICKEN RANCHER WROTE A CRIME NOVEL

By Bill Pronzini

Petaluma, California, is my home town. It's a small place some forty miles north of San Francisco, built around the upper reaches of a salt-water estuary that was called Petaluma Creek when I was a kid but has since been upgraded, by a 1959 act of the state legislature, to Petaluma River. I spent the first twenty-two years of my life within the town's dusty confines.

Until the 1980s, Petaluma was an agricultural town – the center of a chicken- and dairy-ranching area. Milk and milk products are still a staple of its economy, but the chicken-and-egg business, for a variety of reasons, is pretty much a thing of the past. This is sad for historical as well as economic reasons. Time was, Petaluma's whole identity was tied up in chickens and eggs. It used to bill itself, with considerable justification, as "The Egg Basket of the World": During its boom years in the early 1900s, its farms and hatcheries produced and shipped millions of eggs annually (22 million dozen in 1920). It was so poultry-oriented that many things in town were named for or after chickens: the local semi-pro baseball and football teams were the Leghorns, for instance, and there was once a Chicken Pharmacy that made it into *Ripley's Believe It or Not.* The Chamber of Commerce even employed a "Welcome Chicken" (later "Chicken Lady") – an individual who would dress up in a chicken suit, attend parades and other civic functions, and welcome, new families into the area. This phenomenon continued into the seventies, as witness the following ad which appeared in the *San Francisco Chronicle* in 1971 : "Chicken Lady Wanted: Must dress up like a hen, cluck greeting to Petaluma newcomers. No experience needed, but prefer woman who will put civic interest ahead of personal life." (You think I'm making all this up, right? Skeptics are invited to e-mail for proof.)

Since the decline of the chicken-and-egg business, Petaluma's chief claim to fame – aside from its present lamentable status as a trendy "bedroom community" for Bay Area commuters, which has swelled the population from around 12,000 when I was a kid to over 40,000 at the last census – is as the birthplace of the annual World Wristwrestling Championship. Otherwise, its celebrity status is pretty thin. Actor Lloyd Bridges went to school in Petaluma; and character actor and "B" director Myron Healey was born there. (My mother, who attended school at the same time as Bridges, said that he was called "Snotnose," for obvious reasons. However, since my mother was prone to hyperbole, you should take this with several grains of salt.) Poet Arthur Winfield Knight also hails from Petaluma. Its next most famous native-son writer is probably me, which ought to tell you plenty about the town's literary heritage.

In the spring of 1960, when I was still an impressionable teen-ager, a middle-aged Petaluma chicken rancher named Hy Silver published his first and only mystery novel. Its title was *Bogus Lover,* and it caused quite a stir locally – a bigger stink in certain circles than all of Hy's chickens combined.

What fueled the flap was the presence in the novel of four elements: homosexuality and transvestitism, four-letter words (this was 1960, remember), Mike Hammer-type violence, and steamy sex (heterosexual). *Bogus Lover* has its fair share of all four, though all are tame by today's standards. Nor are any of the four particularly integral or necessary to the storyline.

The latter fact was the centerpiece of Hy's defense: He claimed that very little of the controversial stuff was his. He would never write such things, he said in an interview. He was as horrified as anybody when he received his author's copies and found all that crap cluttering up his book.

Hy's version went like this: A few years earlier, after painstakingly writing the novel, he'd sent it around to a bunch of publishers and garnered an equal number of rejection slips. So then he'd shipped the manuscript to one of those individuals who advertise in *Writer's Digest*, offering for various fees such "literary counselling" services as evaluation, editing, and, if necessary, collaboration. The literary counsellor Hy chose informed him that what his book needed to make it salable was some revision and "spicing up," which he, the agent, would attend to for a fee and a cut of the proceeds. Hy, being an eager novice, readily agreed. The agent made the changes and insertions, which Hy said he never saw, and then sold the book to a Chicago-based paperback publisher called Newsstand Library. Hy had never heard of them, but the important thing to him was that he was about to become a Published Author. He didn't even know that his original title (I forget what it was) had been changed to *Bogus Lover* until his copies arrived. It was then and only then that he realized Newsstand Library was a softcore-porn publisher and that his literary counsellor had sold him down a river of sleaze.

Some Petalumans believed Hy's version; some didn't. (I do to this day, having had a little experience with literary counsellors myself over the years.) Some treated the whole thing as a sly joke, some thought it was tempest in a teapot, and the bluenoses used it to illustrate their theories on moral decay and the imminent collapse of Western civilization. As for me, I found it all very exciting. Not the controversy; I didn't much care about that. No, what excited the young mystery fan and fledgling author was this: I knew Hy Silver. I actually *knew* a genuine, honest-to-God mystery writer!

In those days bowling was one of my recreational activities. It was also one of Hy's. My mother worked at the local lanes, which allowed me to hang out there with full parental approval, not to mention a discount on every game I bowled. Some evenings, to make pocket money, I would keep score for league matches (electronic scorekeeping was only a rumor in Petaluma back then); and one of the leagues I worked was the one in which Hy bowled. I didn't know him well, just to say hello to. But I did know him. (I even remember, after nearly thirty years, that he was short and stocky and wore a mustache and was left-handed.) So when I heard about his mystery novel being published, I immediately sought out a copy. There was a newsstand in town that I frequented regularly, to buy Gold Medal and Avon and Ace Double paperbacks and such digest magazines as *Manhunt* as they came out. The owner knew me and wasn't surprised when I sauntered up to him with a copy of *Bogus Lover* in hand; it was obvious to me even then that he thought I was a pretty strange kid. Not that that stopped him from selling me Hy Silver's book, even though technically I was under age. I took it home and consumed it in one long gulp.

Setting: San Francisco. Hero and narrator: ex-cop Anthony Ceaser (sic), owner and operator of a pinball-machine sales and service outfit called Ceaser Amusement Co., who packs a .45 in a shoulder holster to protect himself on collection days. Sidekicks: a 6'3" machinist called Shorty and a ubiquitous taxi driver and sage named Joe Pinsky. Other characters: a murdered homosexual piano player, one "Cookie"; the leader of a gang of armored-car robbers, "Angel Face" Lawrence; a sinister Chinese import-export dealer, Charlie Yee, whose speech patterns are closer to Caspar Gutman's than to Charlie Chan's; a beautiful (and willing) mystery lady named Lorna; a beautiful (and will-ing) cocktail waitress and ear-nibbler named Peggy; a crooked lawyer; assorted cops, thugs, and bartenders; and, for good mea-sure, a chicken-ranching couple from Petaluma. Central plot ele-ment: The search for half a million bucks in unrecovered loot from an armored-car heist.

Sample dialogue:

"Do you think sex will ever replace night baseball?"

"Are you trying to throw me a curve?"

"I might be, baby, but I don't know where in the world you'd put another one."

More sample dialogue:

"... I could have sworn your mother was a mare. Only a mare could give birth to a horse's ass like you."

Still more sample dialogue (proving that Tony Ceaser is really just a sentimental slob at heart):

"When this is all over, Lorna – and I hope to God it's soon – I'm going to take you down to Carmel. There's a little place I know of, where you can hear the ocean come roaring in like a thousand freight trains and then when it's spent itself on the beach you can hear it tiptoeing away like a satisfied lover. You can look straight ahead for a hundred years and see nothing but water and sky and you can use that hundred years to taste just one kiss."

If, from the foregoing, you deduce that *Bogus Lover* is a dog, you are so right. It is in fact a woofer of Alternative Classic dimensions. Be that as it may, the uncritical 17-year-old fledgling writer was captivated by every word of it.

The next time Hy Silver's league bowled, I made sure I was in attendance. And even though there was a crowd of people around, I marshalled my courage and walked right up to Hy and said, "Mr. Silver, I just want you to know that I read *Bogus Lover* and I think it's terrific. I really learned a lot from it."

From the look on his face, you'd have thought I said, "Mr. Silver, your fly is open."

He glanced around furtively, mumbled something, gave me a weak smile, and sidled off. Thereafter, whenever he saw me, an oddly nervous expression crossed his face and he avoided contact. I was puzzled and a little hurt at the time (I chalked it up to "artistic temperament"), but these many years later I think I know why he reacted as he did. He'd had enough of the flap over his book; he didn't want any more hassles. And I had delivered my praise in a loud voice in front of witnesses.

Poor old Hy was afraid of being accused of contributing to the delinquency of a minor!

Bill Pronzini has published 90 novels, including seven in collaboration with his wife, Marcia Muller, and 46 in his popular "Nameless Detective" series. He is also the author of four nonfiction books, 20 collections of short stories, and scores of uncollected articles, essays, and book reviews; and he has edited or coedited numerous anthologies. His work has been translated into nineteen languages and published in nearly thirty countries. He has received six nominations for MWA's Edgar Allan Poe award, as well as three Shamus Awards, two for best novel. In 1987, he received the Lifetime Achievement Award from the Private Eye Writers of America and in 2008 he was named Mystery Writers of America Grand Master, the organization's highest award. This essay was originally published in *Mystery Scene Magazine* in March 1990.

CHAPTER ONE

I T WAS MONDAY. I didn't have to look at a calendar to tell it was Monday. I could tell from the worried look on Shorty's face. But then, Shorty always looked worried. I could tell, also, from the taste in my mouth—sweat socks and limburger cheese—the result of a very large week-end with a very small brunette.

The day dragged on, as Monday always does, and it was after midnight by the time Shorty and I headed for Big Sam's on Columbus Avenue in San Francisco's North Beach section. The fog had started to roll in as Shorty and I walked up the street and the cool moist air felt good going down.

I always tried to make Big Sam's the last stop on the route because I could relax there and Cookie, the piano player, knew all my favorite pieces. Big Sam's had a neon sign jutting out over the entrance. Attached to the bottom of it was another sign, this one made of canvas and announcing simply, "AT THE PIANO BAR—JACQUES COQUETTE." The fog and the salt air had taken its toll so that now the legend was barely visible. Big Sam had wanted to remove the canvas long ago, but Cookie (no one ever called him Jacques) wouldn't let him. Cookie felt that the sign was his last remaining claim to fame. Big Sam had to humor him—good piano men are hard to find.

Shorty had to duck his head as we passed the sign. His gangling six-foot-three stringbean frame wasn't built for low bridges. Unfortunately, I didn't have that problem. Shorty was seven inches my senior.

When we got inside I headed directly for the piano bar while Shorty went to the pinball machine to clean out the bulging box of pretty nickels. Cookie spotted me as I walked in and started playing, "Just A Gigolo." Peggy, the cocktail waitress, served me a bourbon and soda almost before I sat down. The drink was cold but her smile was warm. Real warm. Peggy was a good kid but she had only one thing on her mind—and you didn't have to be a mind reader to tell what it was. She nibbled on my ear as she bent over me to set my drink down.

"Taste good?" I asked.

"M-m-m," she said, "but I'd like it better if it was filled with anchovies and mushrooms."

"That's fattening," I said, "you'd better watch your figure."

She said, "I'd rather have you watch it."

The conversation might have developed into something interesting but Cookie interrupted. "What would you like to hear?"

"How about "Little Girl Blue"?", I said. It was one of my favorites and Cookie enjoyed playing it because he claimed to have known Larry Hart personally and dropped his name frequently when we discussed music. I relaxed with my elbows on top of the piano, sipping my drink, ready to enjoy Cookie's flawless arrangement. The enjoyment didn't last long. He played like he had twelve thumbs.

He made so many mistakes that several times he had to stop and start over again. I could see him frown all the way to the top of his head where his hair was thinning. He played with one hand half the time so that he could hold a handkerchief in his other bony hand and mop up the perspiration. He finally brought "Little Girl Blue" to a tortured ending and sat huddled on the piano bench looking even smaller than he actually was.

"What's the matter, Cookie," I asked, "have a fight with one of your boy friends?"

"No, nothing like that," he said. "Christ, I need a drink." I motioned to Peggy and pointed to Cookie. She brought him a drink which he downed gratefully.

"Thanks, Tony," he mumbled, "you're very sweet." He got up and came toward me. He looked around the room nervously. The place was practically deserted. Big Sam, who didn't get that name because he was a midget, stood behind the bar ponderously polishing glasses. Peggy was studying the numbers on the juke box and Shorty was counting and rolling nickels. There was only one other customer in the place and he was sitting hunched over the far end of the bar with his back to us.

"Tony," he said at last, "I'm in terrible trouble. I need help."

"What's the problem, chum?" I asked. Cookie was always in terrible trouble. He had a talent for over-dramatizing. I liked Cookie, but sometimes when he had too much to drink he was a terrible bore. He would either talk incessantly about his sordid love life or he would become belligerent like a little game cock ready to take on the biggest rooster in the barnyard.

He started to tell me something then changed his mind. "I could use another drink."

I bought him another drink and Peggy helped herself to some more ear when she served it.

"Don't you ever get tired of doing that?", I asked Peggy.

She looked at me through half-closed eyes. "When I get tired I go to bed."

"Be sure to bundle up," I said, "the nights are getting colder."

"But I'm so warm-blooded," she answered, "I sleep in the raw. How do you sleep?"

"Alone," I said. Peggy went back to the juke box. I turned to Cookie and looked at him inquiringly.

Cookie was staring into his drink. "I'm a sucker," he said morosely. I was about to ask him what kind, but thought better of it.

"Do you want to tell me about it?"

He sipped his drink absently. "I know too much."

"Well, I don't know enough," I said. "Suppose you enlighten me."

"They're out to get me," he said. His slender hands were trembling but I've seen that reaction from too much booze.

"Who's out to get you?"

"I can't tell you."

"For this I had to buy you two drinks? If we're playing riddles, count me out."

He clutched my arm. "But you don't understand—"

I disengaged his hand lest someone get suspicious of our relationship. "How do you expect me to understand something you haven't told me? Now, let's start over—who's out to get you and what for?"

"This is big, Tony, real big. Listen," he said suddenly, "will you hang around until I'm through and then take me home?"

"Oho," I said, "so that's your angle. How many times must I tell you you're not my type? Now go sit down like a good little boy and play me some of that fine piano."

Cookie looked at me with large frightened eyes. "For God's sake, Tony, this is no joke. If you don't help me I may be dead by morning." He sounded so sincere I was beginning to believe him.

I said, "I'm afraid I can't help you until I know what this is all about."

Cookie put his head in his hands and started sobbing quietly. He shuddered, took a deep breath and then dabbed at his eyes with his handkerchief. He was a pathetic sight and I was beginning to feel embarrassed for him. I was glad that the place was empty. Finally, he said, "If I tell you then you'll be in danger, too. They'll kill you if they even suspect you know."

"That may not be easy," I said patting the bulge under my armpit, "I die real hard." I carried the gun for protection on the route and, what's more, I knew how to use it. "Now, what's this all about?"

Cookie swallowed a couple of times. "I'll tell you about it after we get out of here. I can't talk here."

"If you're so damned scared, why don't you call the cops?"

Cookie winced and looked around. "I want to, but—" He stopped talking suddenly, staring past me to the entrance of the bar. I turned around to see what had caught his attention and promptly forgot all about Cookie and his problems. Coming through the doorway was the biggest, most luscious blonde I had ever seen. I like them big, especially in the right places. This one didn't have any wrong places. She was striking but, strangely enough, what attracted my attention most of all was her hair. It wasn't exactly blonde, it was more golden and it sort of cascaded down to her shoulders like a waterfall in the sunset.

She came directly to the piano bar and sat down. Peggy walked over and set a napkin down in front of her. She ordered a bourbon on the rocks and my admiration for her soared a few more points. You don't find many women who can take their liquor straight. I told Peggy to bring me another drink and put both drinks on my tab.

The blonde turned toward me. "I don't usually accept drinks from strangers."

"We can take care of that," I said moving next to her. "My name is Anthony Ceaser. My friends call me Tony. What do your friends call you?"

She stared at me for a full minute. I turned on my most pleasant smile and let her take inventory. What she saw was black wavy hair, blue eyes and a good set of teeth. Most women don't find me too repulsive.

When she spoke again I noticed her voice. It was low and throaty. Sexy. Real sexy. It sent a tingling from the nape of my neck to the base of my spine. She said, "You don't waste much time, do you?"

"I don't have much time to waste and I won't waste yours. I think you're the most beautiful creature I've ever seen. Will you have an affair with me?"

She laughed. Peggy brought our drinks, glared at me and moved away.

"How about it?" I asked.

"What kind of an affair did you have in mind?"

"Oh, nothing sordid," I said. "It would help if I knew your name."

"It's Lorna."

"All right, Lorna, first we'll set the proper mood." I turned to Cookie who was seated back on the piano bench. "Play us something romantic."

He gave me an anguished look and started playing. It was horrible. By the law of averages he should have hit a few right notes but he wasn't breaking the law, he was mangling it. I tossed him a bill and told him to buy himself a drink and play something on the juke box. He took the bill and went to the bar.

Lorna said, "What's the matter with Cookie? I've never heard him play like that before."

"He's got a problem," I said, "but so have I."

"Oh? What's your problem?"

"It's a psychological one. I've got an overwhelming desire to take you in my arms and—"

"It sounds more biological. Try hormones."

"You're fighting me."

"Not yet, but I will if your impulses get any stronger. Do you usually behave this way?"

"Of course not," I said, "it's just the way you affect me."

"Perhaps I'd better leave."

"Not without me. Do you live near here?"

"Not too far."

"Do you come here often?"

"Sometimes, I think, too often."

I tried a new tack. "Do you think sex will ever replace night baseball?"

"Are you trying to throw me a curve?"

"I might be," I said, "but I don't know where in the world you'd put another one."

She laughed. Even when she laughed she was sexy. Our conversation was interrupted by Shorty, who tapped me on the shoulder.

He said, "All set, boss, let's blow."

I could have killed him on the spot except that I'd be out the best mechanic in the business. Shorty could get a pinball machine to do everything except cook breakfast—and he was working on that angle.

I said, "You run along, Shorty. I've got a little unfinished business to attend to here."

Lorna said, "Don't let me detain you."

"How do you expect me to leave?" Shorty asked. "You've got the keys to the car."

"Just walk down one block and pick up a cab. Put it on the expense account."

"Yeah," said Shorty gloomily. "I thought you were beat from the week-end and wanted to rest tonight. This isn't doing your ulcer any good."

Shorty's motherly instincts weren't easily curbed. I was afraid if he hung around much longer he would queer the whole deal. I slipped off of my stool, grabbed Shorty's arm and guided him to the front door. "Now be a good boy and run along," I told him.

"You ought to come, too, boss," he said. "That dame looks like trouble."

"Yeah," I said, unable to suppress a leer, "just the kind of trouble I like. See you tomorrow," and with that I propelled him gently through the front door.

I went back inside. Lorna was sitting where I had left her. I don't know why, but I was afraid she might disappear. Cookie was playing the pinball machine and Big Sam was still polishing glasses. For a guy who was doing no business, he sure had a lot of dirty glasses.

"Now, where were we?" I said to Lorna as I sat down.

"You were just getting ready to proposition me."

"Oh, was I? I thought I did that already. I must be losing my touch. What was your answer?"

"I didn't give you one."

"Are you going to?"

"My, you're persistent."

"It's not that at all," I said, "it's just that you're reluctant.

"Not reluctant," she said, "merely cautious. Don't forget, I hardly know you."

"I'm not hard to know. Would you go out with me if I promised to be a perfect gentleman?"

She smiled. "What fun would that be?"

"Don't worry," I said, "I don't always keep my promises. How about it?"

"What have you got in mind?"

"We'll go out and get a bite to eat and then we can play photography."

"What's that?"

"We sit in a dark room and see what develops."

"I might be persuaded to take on a little food but I don't know if I'll like the games you play."

"If you haven't tried it, don't knock it," I said. "Let's go." I started to get up.

"Wait a minute," she said, "not so fast."

I sat down. "What's the hitch?"

"I don't want people to get the wrong idea."

I looked around the room. "What people?"

"There's Big Sam and Peggy and Cookie. They all know me. I come here quite often."

"So?"

"So, I want to maintain my self-respect."

"You'll lose it if you go out with me?"

"I don't mean that. But if I walk out of here with you I'll look like a cheap pick-up."

"Honey, you couldn't look cheap if you tried. You've got too much class."

"Thank you, but I know how I'd feel."

"Then what do you suggest?"

She thought a minute. "Suppose I meet you somewhere?"

"Where?"

"Anywhere, as long as we don't leave together."

"I'll buy that. Where shall we meet?"

"You leave first and wait for me out back. I'll wait a respectable few minutes and then I'll come back and meet you. That way nobody will be the wiser and I can keep my reputation intact."

I said, "Okay, doll." She reached over and squeezed my hand and gave me a smile that was full of promise.

It wasn't until I was out the door and halfway to the rear of the building that I remembered Cookie's frantic plea to see him home. But I quickly dismissed it from my mind as an alcohol induced problem created by Cookie's peculiar social situation.

I walked down the street alongside Big Sam's until I came to an alley that ran behind the building. I stood on the corner and glanced at my watch. It was a quarter to two. I started pacing back and forth restlessly. Five minutes went by. Ten. I was beginning to get the feeling that I was being stood up. I decided to wait five more minutes and then go home.

I thought how nice the bed would feel. It had been a rough week-end and I could stand the rest. Then I thought about running my fingers through that golden hair. I was so absorbed in my reverie that I didn't hear the footsteps behind me until it was too late. I might not have heard them anyway for they were very stealthy steps. I started to turn around when it felt like the building had tumbled onto my head.

When I came to I was lying on my back and there was a terrific throbbing in my head. There was also a pressure on my chest. I raised my chest. I raised my head and saw that there was a body lying across mine, face down. There was something familiar about it. I reached under the body to roll it off. My hands felt something warm and sticky. I struggled to a sitting position and saw that I was holding a very dead Cookie in my arms. His head hung down in grotesque position and there was a large stain on the front of his shirt.

I got up as I heard footsteps running down the side street. I pulled my gun and had it ready but I relaxed when I saw it was a patrolman. He shined his flashlight in my face and then down to Cookie's inert body.

"What the hell is going on here?" he demanded.

"That's what I'd like to know," I said. "Somebody konked me on the head and I came to with a dead friend draped all over me."

The patrolman knelt down to examine Cookie's body. "He's dead, all right. Look's like he's been shot." He straightened up and suddenly whipped his gun out of his holster. He pointed it right at my heart.

"What's the big idea?" I said.

"That's what I'd like to know," he answered. "Let me have your gun."

"Sure," I said, "it hasn't been fired in months. I just carry it for protection." I grabbed the barrel with my other hand to hand it to him butt first but I dropped it. The barrel was hot!

CHAPTER TWO

BRIGHT SUNLIGHT FILTERED through the bars of my cell. I had slept fitfully through the night, or what was left of it by the time they finished questioning me. When my violently reacting ulcer wasn't keeping me awake, the acrid smell of dried vomit was. I tried to take my mind off my discomfort by silently reviewing the chain of events that had brought me there. I thought about Mac, Lt. "Mac" McGovern, now in homicide and of the great times we had had together when I was on the force. And thinking back to those happier days it was impossible to keep the painful memories of Alice from flooding my thoughts.

Alice and I had been childhood sweethearts. There had never been any doubt in either of our minds that someday we would get married. And we did when I had a delay enroute before shipping out to the Pacific during the war. Our honeymoon was altogether too short and so was our marriage. I had been out of the army for less than a year when Alice was killed by a hit and run driver. That really broke me up. But when the police failed to apprehend the murderer, I guess I went to pieces. I quit the force and started some man-sized drinking. I never forgave the police force for not finding the stinking murderer and I never forgave the world for giving me Alice and then taking her away.

I might have ended up on a slab in the morgue or flat on my back in a flea-bitten rat-trap down on Third and Howard with the rest of the winos if it hadn't been for Shorty. Shorty and I became acquainted at Big Sam's. He stopped in for a beer one night as I was winding up an alcoholic extravaganza that had been going on for five or six days. He irked me because he was so tall so I tried to cut him to my size. The fight ended after two wild swings—mine—and one punch—Shorty's.

He took me home that night and sobered me up. I stayed at his place for two days just regaining some of the strength I had dissipated away over the previous week. Shorty didn't lecture or preach to me. He merely set an example of how a human being should behave. I felt so ashamed of myself after two days of his solicitous treatment that when he suggested that I apply for a job at the machine shop where he worked, I jumped at the chance.

It was back breaking labor but I enjoyed every minute of it. I worked off my frustration and sweated out my bitterness. And since I wasn't giving all of my money to the friendly bartenders, I managed to accumulate enough to buy a pinball machine route. Shorty came to work for me shortly afterwards. I offered him a partnership but he refused it. He said he didn't want the responsibility but I think he refused because he wanted me to regain all of the selfesteem I had lost through my debauchery. However, he never stopped acting like the little mother hen trying to protect her chick from the evils of the big bad world. Sometimes he managed to get on my nerves but it's a good feeling to know someone cares about what happens to you.

My reverie was interrupted by a gruff voice that said. "Come on, Bud, McGovern wants to see you." The cell door swung open and I was escorted up to Mac's office. He was talking on the phone when I walked in so he motioned me to sit down. He hung up the phone and offered me a cigarette.

"Well, Tony," he said, running a hand through his sandy colored hair, "your story checks out."

"Did you think it wouldn't?"

"No, not for a minute, but I had to lock you up. Routine—you know that."

"Sure, sure," I said, "I needed the rest anyway. Now tell me, what did you find out?"

"First of all, before I forget, you can pick up your personal effects at the desk."

"What about my gun?"

"We have to hold it, at least until the inquest. Cookie had two slugs in his chest and ballistics prove they were fired from your gun."

"That adds up," I said.

"But the paraffin test showed that you hadn't fired the gun."

"I told you that last night."

"But we have to make sure. What good would your testimony be if we didn't substantiate it with the facts? There's another interesting bit of evidence our investigation disclosed."

"What's that?"

"According to the powder tattoo we've determined that the shots were fired from a distance of about four feet. But according to the angle in which the bullets entered his body, they would have to have been fired by a midget."

"Unless Cookie was flat on his back and the killer stood over him. Did you find any marks on him showing that he had been knocked down?"

"We did better than that. We were able to determine that he was dead before the bullets entered his body."

My ears perked up. "How's that?"

"The actual cause of death was from a broken neck."

I gave out a low whistle. "So somebody was trying to set me up for a patsy."

"Exactly. The bump on your head bears that out. The size of the laceration and its location rules out any possibility that it was self-inflected."

"Why should I want to knock myself out? Isn't that kind of ridiculous?"

"It would appear ridiculous unless you had a motive for killing Cookie and you did it in such a way to make it look like you were being framed. Captain Coletti still hasn't ruled out that possibility."

"Coletti!" I said, "I'm not surprised."

"Nick figures you could have done it easily with the aid of an accomplice."

"Do you mind telling me how?"

"Simple enough. You kill Cookie by breaking his neck. You have your accomplice slug you, then fire two shots into Cookie's body with you gun. You get picked up and brought to headquarters screaming you've been framed and insisting on a paraffin test to show that you didn't fire the fatal bullets."

"But they turned out not to be fatal."

"We found that out. I'm just telling you Coletti's thinking on this thing. It doesn't necessarily mean that I agree with him."

I remembered Captain Nick Coletti very well. He was in charge of the investigation of Alice's death. He refused to assign me to the case at the time and the newspapers got wind of the story. They rode him unmercifully, especially when he failed to solve the case. He was convinced that I leaked the story to the papers and he swore to get even with me.

"So if the great captain still suspects me, why are you letting me go?"

"We don't have enough to hold you on and he knows it. Everyone in the immediate area was questioned and no one remembers seeing anyone leave the scene of the crime. That alone rules out the accomplice possibility."

"I hate to stick my neck back into the noose, but wouldn't that also rule out the possibility of someone besides me killing Cookie?"

"You have hit upon one of the puzzling aspects of this case. But I'll scratch around until I figure that one out. In the meantime, I want you to know that if Coletti can book you on this thing, he will, so just watch your step."

"Thanks for the advice but I think I can take care of myself."

"You didn't do such a hot job last night."

"I'm just a sucker for big blondes, let's face it."

"Any idea who she is?"

"I told you last night all I know about her is her name. But I'll find her, don't you worry, and when I get through with her it'll take more than a good plastic surgeon to straighten her out."

"How can you be sure she had anything to do with it?"

I grinned. "Even a stupid cop like you ought to be able to figure that one out. I wouldn't have been back in that alley if it wasn't for her."

It was Mac's turn to grin. "Maybe she wasn't buying what you were selling. Maybe it was the only way she could get rid of you."

"Yeah," I said, "and maybe it was just a coincidence that I got slugged and somebody pumped the two slugs from my gun into Cookie's body. Maybe you'll buy that fairy tale but I won't."

Mac lit a cigarette and leaned back in his chair. "You were a cop long enough to know that circumstantial evidence can be highly misleading. But I won't argue the point now." He pulled out a ten dollar bill and threw it onto the desk. "Ever see one of these before?"

I picked it up and examined it. "Are you kidding? I was carrying a pocketful of them last night when your boys brought me in."

"Not like this one, you weren't. If you did, you'd be in trouble now—real trouble."

I examined the bill more closely. "What's so special about this one?" I held it up to the light. "If it's a phony, I'd sure love to have the plates."

"Oh, it's no phony," Mac said, "but it's a hot piece of merchandise. A few of these in your possession would almost guarantee you a one-way trip to the gas chamber. Unless, of course, you had some pretty good answers."

I still didn't get it. "What's so special about it?"

Mac looked at me through narrowed eyelids. "Do you remember that armored car robbery a couple of years back?"

I thought for a moment. "Yeah," I said, "a half a million bucks that was never recovered and the guard was killed."

"Do you remember how he was killed?"

"Sure, he was shot. No, wait a minute," I said, as all of a sudden it struck me. "Why—he had his neck broken!"

"Exactly," Mac said.

"But what about this ten spot? Was this part of the loot?"

"Right again," said Mac, "we found it on Cookie's body."

"Are you trying to say that Cookie was mixed up in that caper?"

"Even a stupid ex-cop like you should be able to see the tie-in."

"But Cookie was no criminal," I said. "He may have been a little mixed up about his sex, but—"

Mac cut me off. "Let me refresh your memory and fill you in on the details. We caught the gang that pulled the job."

"Yeah, I remember," I said, "you didn't waste much time, either. But you couldn't find the money."

"That's right, and the gang wouldn't tell us where it was."

"Of course they wouldn't. As I recall, they all maintained they were innocent. They weren't about to furnish you with the only piece of evidence that was irrefutable."

"It didn't make any difference," Mac continued, "they were all convicted and sentenced to die in the gas chamber at San Quentin. Now, what else do you remember about the trial?"

"Not too much," I said.

"The leader of the gang was a fellow named Alfred Lawrence."

"Yeah," I said, "the newspapers nicknamed him 'Angel Face.' Alfred 'Angel Face' Lawrence, but Angel Face made a spectacular escape from the courthouse and hasn't been found since."

"We have every reason to believe he's still in the city. One reason is the money. We've got a complete list of serial numbers of the stolen money. It's hot. Real hot. We believe the money is stashed away here in the city and that Angel Face is trying to figure an angle to unload it."

"What makes you think so?" I asked.

"Because several of the bills have turned up recently. And do you know where?" I shook my head. "All of them have turned up in North Beach."

"Haven't you been able to trace the guy who's passing them?"

"No. Whoever is passing them is too clever. They're all passed during business rush hours in markets and in restaurants. You can't expect a clerk to remember all the people who hand him ten or twenty dollar bills, especially if he has no reason to be on the lookout.

"Now, we've kept this thing strictly quiet. We want our pigeon to think he's getting away with it."

"I got it," I said, "you want him to get a little reckless. But how do you tie Angel Face in with last night's caper?"

"I think that Cookie was tied in some way. He was either being used to pass the bills or he knew something. From what you told me of his conversation last night I'm inclined to think he stumbled onto something and he had to be silenced—permanently."

I lit a fresh cigarette from the butt of the one I was smoking. I looked Mac straight in the eyes and said, "Why are you telling me all of this?"

"Because," he said, "I know you. I know you well enough to know that you'll go sticking your neck out far enough for Angel Face to get his hands around it. And that's all brother. Now, will you take a little good advice?"

"No," I said, "but I'll listen."

"Keep your nose out of this."

I waited for more but Mac said nothing. He just sat there staring at me. "Is that all?"

"That's all. I'm telling you as a police officer and," here his voice softened, "as a friend."

"Okay," I said, "now let me tell you something. It took me a long time to get over Alice. A helluva long time. It still gets me when I think about it so I try not to think about it. And then this happens. A harmless little fairy gets knocked off by a dirty rat.

It's not the same rotten bastard that got Alice, but they're all the same. If I get to this one before you do, there won't be much of him left. I don't care how tough he is. And then, and only then, maybe it'll even up the score just a little bit."

Mac didn't say anything for a minute. He let out a big sigh and fooled around with his pencil making doodles on his blotter. When he spoke, he spoke so low I had to strain to hear him.

"I was afraid you'd feel that way." He stuck his hand out. "Take care of yourself, Tony. It won't be the same town without you."

CHAPTER THREE

MAC HAD A SQUAD CAR take me to where I had left my car the night before. It was parked about a block away from Big Sam's and I had told Mac that if there was a ticket on it I was going to shove it down his throat. Only I didn't say "throat."

I always do my best thinking when I'm riding in a car so I started analyzing the events of the last night. I had been waiting out in back for between ten and fifteen minutes. During that time someone had broken Cookie's neck, dragged or carried his body to the back of the building, slugged me and shot Cookie with my gun. But how? The murderer couldn't have done away with Cookie inside Big Sam's. Too many witnesses. And if he had waited for Cookie in front of the place that would have been just as bad—maybe worse. Columbus is a pretty busy street, even at two in the morning. So where and how was Cookie killed?

I knew that Mac would question all the people who were in the joint the night before but they could sing him a lullaby and Mac wouldn't know the difference. I would. There had to be a logical explanation for what happened and I intended to find it out.

When the squad car let me off I walked back up to Big Sam's but I didn't go inside. Instead I walked around to the rear of the building where I had been the night before. I didn't expect to find anything for I was certain that Mac's boys had by this time gone over the area pretty carefully. I found the approximate place I was standing when I had been slugged and then I tried to determine how the killer had approached me. There seemed to be only one possible way and that was all the way up the alley behind me. But that would have been too risky for the killer. It was a long way to come without being detected. There had to be some other way and I wasn't long in finding it. It was the back entrance to Big Sam's. It would have been easy for the killer to slip out the back way, walk the few steps to where I was standing, fit me out for a concussion and—here I stopped. Where was Cookie all this time? There was only one way to find out.

I took the back entrance into Big Sam's. The back door opened up into a hallway. Right near the back door there was a pay phone in a little cubicle. Adjacent to this was the ladies room. Across from the ladies room, the mens room. I walked through the hallway into the bar. The place was empty except for Tom, the relief bartender. I couldn't figure out if Big Sam's was the cleanest or the dirtiest bar in town because Tom was standing behind the bar polishing glasses.

"Where's Big Sam?" I asked Tom. Tom became so startled at the sound of my voice he almost dropped the glass he was working on.

"Where did you come from, Tony? I didn't see you come in."

"I didn't come in the front way and you didn't answer my question."

"Oh, you want Big Sam? He's home I guess. When he works the night shift he don't usually get here until six, sometimes a little before. Why, what's up?"

I ignored his question. "Know anything about a big blonde that comes in here?" He creased his brow in concentration. For him, I knew it was a supreme effort. I tried to help him. "She's a couple of inches taller than I am, built like a freight train loaded in the right places. ... "

Tom smiled. "Oh, yeah, that one. Nice, huh?"

"What's her name?"

"Uh, uh, Lorna. Yeah, that's it Lorna."

"Her last name?"

"I dunno."

"Where does she live?"

"Around here somewhere, I guess."

I know when I'm licked so I turned and headed for the front door. I didn't get three steps when Tom called me back.

"Say, Tony, there's something wrong with the pinball machine."

"What's wrong with it?"

"I dunno, but it won't take no nickels. It's stuck."

"Okay," I said, "I'll send Shorty over to fix it."

I was anxious to get out of my wrinkled, blood-stained clothes and take a nice hot shower but I thought I'd better check into the office first. I knew that Shorty would be worried about me and a phone call wouldn't appease him. My office wasn't much of an office. It was an old store on Bay Street, not too far from Fisherman's Wharf. I had a desk and some filing cabinets in the front and the back was used to store new machines and repair the old ones. I had one other fixture in the office. Her name was Wanda.

Wanda was a combination bookkeeper, secretary, receptionist. She also had a few other combinations working for her. Wanda was a lot of big things wrapped in a small package. She had the kind of legs that chemists at DuPont must have been dreaming of when they invented nylon. And the sweaters she wore constantly managed to outline and accentuate a full rounded bosom that defied gravity. I wouldn't have kept her on the job for a minute if she wasn't so damned efficient. She was too distracting. I was afraid that someday a sucker would come along and she would sell him the cottage small routine because there was no other way to score with this gal. And I was afraid that sucker might be me.

When I got to the office, Wanda was so engrossed with a run in her stockings she didn't notice me. I stood there admiring the exquisite contour of her calf and the full-bodied voluptuousness of her rounded thigh. A ribbon of pink flesh showed between the folds of her skirt and the top of her stocking.

"What time is the second show?" I said. "I wouldn't want to miss it."

She pulled her skirt down quickly as her pretty face became suffused with a reddish glow. "Tony, don't you ever do that again."

I sat down on the edge of the desk facing her. She said, "You startled me." I put my hands on her shoulders. "You know you have no right—" she began. I smothered the rest of her sentence with my lips. Her mouth was soft and moist and warm. She finally pushed me away.

"This is not what I'm getting paid for," she said.

"You wanna bet?"

She looked at me sharply. "Tony, you look terrible. You look like you've slept in that suit."

"As a matter fact, I did," I said as I noticed Shorty's grave features peering at me from the doorway of the back room.

"What happened?" Shorty asked, bringing his lank frame into full view.

"I've been a guest of the city," I said, "and the accommodations leave much to be desired."

"What were you doing in jail?" Shorty demanded.

I briefly recounted the events of the past evening. When I finished, Shorty said, "I told you that blonde looked like trouble."

"She'll find out what trouble is when I get my hands on her," I said.

"But how are you going to find her if you know nothing about her but her name?" Wanda asked. "And only her first name at that."

"That's where you come in," I said. "The most striking thing about her, besides her height, is her hair. The color was too uniform to be natural and the hair itself too well groomed and highly stylized to have been done at home. So what does that indicate."

"Regular visits to a beauty salon," said Wanda. "That's easy."

"Right," I said. "But the rest may not be so easy. I want you to get the yellow pages of the phone book and start calling every beauty salon in town. Pick out the ones in this area first and if you don't get any results then call the rest of them."

"But what do I say? Do I tell them I'm looking for a tall blonde and describe her, or ... "

"No, they'll get suspicious. They'll want to know who you are and why you want the information. It's too risky. But if you tell them a perfectly innocuous story about why you are trying to locate her, they'll probably bend over backwards trying to help."

"And I suppose you have such a story ready in that fertile little brain of yours?"

"Try this one on for size. Tell them you were in their salon a week or so ago and you borrowed a fountain pen from this very tall blonde. I'll write out a description for you. Then tell them you thought you had returned it but when you were cleaning out your handbag this morning you found it. You must have put it there inadvertently. Put on a scene about how awful you feel and how you'd like to return it personally. If you do hit paydirt but they want you to bring the pen to the salon so that they can return it, tell them you would like to deliver it personally so that you can explain the situation to the blonde. Now have you got all that."

Wanda nodded. "It seems simple enough. I think I can handle it."

Shorty, who had been listening intently, could restrain himself no longer. "Boss," he began, "why do you want to get yourself all mixed up in something that's none of your business?"

"Somebody made it my business," I said, rubbing the knot on the back of my head. "Before I get through they're going to wish they never heard of Tony Ceaser." I felt the blood begin pounding in my temples. I felt a film closing over my eyes, a film of hate so intense that for a moment I couldn't see anything except the faceless body of a murdering rat I was going to track down. And when I did, he was going to die. He was going to die the same way Cookie died, only he was going to suffer first.

I shut my eyes tight to blot out the scene. When I opened them again I saw such a look of motherly concern on Shorty's face that I had to laugh. "Shorty, you'd better hop into the pick-up and scoot over to Big Sam's. Something's wrong with our machine." Immediately, Shorty's attitude changed. This was something he could understand and sink his teeth into. And it showed him I hadn't forgotten that I still had a business to run.

He gave me that big lop-sided grin. "Okay, Boss, I'm on my way."

I turned and saw that Wanda was already poring over the telephone book. So I kissed her on the back of her pretty neck and headed out the front door.

My stomach growled in distress over its recent neglect and my skin felt itchy and crawly from its long confinement. A hot shower and a steaming cup of black coffee had a lot of appeal for me but I had one stop to make first.

I headed the car back up Bay, past Columbus a couple of blocks and turned off. I drove until I came to a series of apartments that once were fashionable but had since come into a state of obsolescence and disrepair. I parked my car in front of an apartment house that boasted of a somewhat shredded awning as its one remaining claim to distinction. I found the button I wanted and pressed it. I received no immediate answering buzz so I pushed the button down and kept it down until after a few minutes I finally got response from the front door. I went in and walked the narrow flight of stairs to the second floor. I found the apartment I was looking for and rapped on the door.

A feminine voice said, "Just a minute," and then the door was opened. Peggy, Big Sam's cocktail waitress was standing there clutching a quilted robe tightly around her body. When she saw it was me she relaxed and stepped aside for me to enter. As she did, the robe fell away partly at the center graphically reminding me that Peggy liked to sleep in the raw.

"Well, this is certainly a surprise," she said.

"Did I get you up?" I asked innocently, knowing damn well I did.

"Yes, you rat," she said, but she was smiling. "If it was anyone else he'd get a coffee pot thrown at his head."

"An excellent idea," I said. "I like mine hot and black."

"Coming right up," she said in her best cocktail waitress voice.

I followed her into the kitchenette and sat down at the table. I watched her as she efficiently measured out the water and coffee. She had her hair up in curlers but she didn't look quite as horrible as most women do when they first get up in the morning.

"What time did you get in this morning?" I asked casually.

"About three, I guess."

"Then you didn't come right home?"

"No, I stopped by Luigi's for Pizza and coffee."

"Alone?"

"Alone."

"What time did you leave Big Sam's?"

"A little before two. Say, what is this, Tony? I'm flattered by your interest but what gives?"

"Sit down, Peggy." She pulled the opposite chair out and sat down with a puzzled look on her face. I took my pack out, offered her a smoke and took one myself. We lit up and I inhaled deeply.

I looked her straight in the eye and said, "Cookie was killed last night. Murdered."

Her face turned ashen. "Oh, no," she cried. She took a deep breath and another drag on her cigarette. "Who? How?"

"I know how. I think I know who. But I need a lot of answers."

"What happened?" she asked me as the color slowly returned to her face.

"You remember that tall blonde that came in last night?" She nodded her head. "She agreed to let me take her home but she didn't want to be seen leaving with me. Said it would make her look cheap, so she told me to wait for her out back. While I was waiting, someone slugged me and then pumped two slugs from my gun into Cookie. But not before he had broken Cookie's neck."

Peggy got up to turn the fire down under the coffee. "It'll be ready in a minute. Who did it?"

"The best guess is Angel Face Lawrence. Does that name mean anything to you?"

She shook her head. "No," she said. "Should it?"

"Not necessarily. Now, I want you to think back carefully and tell me everything that happened after I left last night. This is very important so try not to make any mistakes."

"I don't understand exactly what you want."

"I want to know every move that every person in the bar made last night after I walked out. Let's start with the blonde. Incidentally, what do you know about her?"

"Not very much. She's been in a few times before but she always comes alone and goes alone and she never talks much. Except maybe to Cookie."

"What did they talk about?"

"I don't know," she said. "They never talked when I was within ear-shot. Although I did hear a snatch of something once, but it didn't make any sense."

I sat up. "What was it?"

She frowned, trying to recall the conversation. "It sounded like. 'Charlie eel go for the deal.' "

"Charlie eel go for the deal?"

"Yes. I guess the only reason I remember it is because it's so silly and it rhymes."

"And you don't know anything else about her? Her name? Where she comes from? Anything at all?" She shook her head slowly.

"What did she do right after I left?" I asked.

"Now let me see. She sat at the piano bar for a while."

"Where was Cookie?"

"I think he was either at the juke box or the pinball machine."

"And Big Sam?"

"Behind the bar."

"Polishing glasses?"

"Polishing glasses."

"What about the guy at the end of the bar. Who was he and what did he do?"

"I really didn't get a good look at him. I don't serve at the bar, just the piano bar and the booths. I think he left shortly after you did."

"The front door or back?"

"To tell the truth, I don't know. I just happened to glance where he was sitting and he was gone. He must have left when I was at the juke box.

"Oh, my gosh," she said abruptly, "the coffee's boiling over." She got up to shut it off and came back with the two chipped cups and saucers. "This isn't exactly the Sheraton-Palace," she said.

"I know," I said, "but the room service here is far superior." She blushed and poured the coffee. It was exactly how I liked it; steaming hot, strong and black. I refused the milk and sugar and we sipped our coffee in silence for a few moments.

"When did the blonde leave?"

"It must have been after I did."

"How's that? Aren't you there until the place is closed?"

"Sometimes, and sometimes when there's not too much doing, Big Sam lets me off a little early."

"So the blonde just sat at the piano bar until you left?"

"No, she went to the powder room and I guess she was still there when I left."

"Did you hear anything unusual after you left the place?"

She thought for a moment. "Come to think of it, I did. Luigi's is only a couple of blocks away so I walked over there. On the way I heard a noise that sounded like a car backfiring. It might have been a gun."

"What time was that?"

"It must have been a couple of minutes before two."

I finished my coffee and got up. "Thanks, Peggy, for the coffee and the information."

She got up and stood next to me. Right next to me. Her robe parted again and she didn't bother closing it. I could see the rounded mounds of her creamy white breasts. She held her face close to mine. Her mouth opened slightly as the tip of her tongue delicately moistened her lips.

"Must you leave right away, Tony?" she asked softly. She rubbed up against me and put her cheek next to mine. She put her arms around me and as she did, her robe fell open and I could feel her warm body fitting into the contours of mine. I tilted her head back and the next moment her lips were hungrily devouring mine in a searching, questioning kiss.

She grabbed my hand and led me into the other room.

"We'll be more comfortable in here," she whispered.

I followed her into the bedroom. What the hell, why not? She was over twenty-one. She stopped and turned at the edge of the bed, let her robe slide to the floor, then lifted her arms to my shoulders.

"You're cute, Tony," she breathed, running her fingers through my hair. "You'll be even cuter when you get a bit more relaxed. Like take off your tie, for a starter."

"I never argue with a lady."

The bed was warm and sweet smelling but I was concentrating on something a lot more interesting than the homelike atmosphere. My hand traveled lightly over her body, savoring each lush curve.

"Mmmmmm," Peggy sighed. She wasn't much of a conversationalist in bed.

Her hips began to sway in slow, rhythmic circles, eager with expectation, then faster until they were undulating to a restless mambo beat.

Our bodies blended and we moved together, the silence broken only by the rubbing of perspiring flesh and Peggy's urgent gasps.

"Tony, now! Now, Tony!"

Later, I slipped into my clothes and left the apartment. The price a guy has to pay for a cup of coffee nowadays is no hardship at all!

CHAPTER FOUR

I DROVE TO MY APARTMENT. I was anxious for that shower but first I had to call the office. The line was busy so I undressed and fixed myself a drink. I don't usually drink early in the day but that day I was feeling a little rocky. I tried the phone a few more times and finally got through.

Wanda's crisp voice announced, "Ceaser Amusement Company."

"Come on up and amuse me, baby."

"Oh, Tony," she said, her voice showing excitement, "I've got some information for you."

"Spill it."

"Well, I started calling all the beauty salons in North Beach and ... "

"Never mind the travelogue, what did you find out?"

Her voice showed pique. I was sorry I was so abrupt with her.

"If I had used that phony story you gave, I wouldn't have found out anything. Right away they wanted to know my name and what day I had my appointment. Obviously, you haven't spent much time in beauty salons."

"Listen, doll, if I didn't have complete confidence in your overwhelming competence I wouldn't have given you the job in the first place. You are the epitome of efficiency, a paragon of virtue, a ... "

"Okay, Tony, okay, you win. Her full name is Lorna Williams and her address ... "

"Wait a minute, until I get a pencil and paper." I found a notebook and a pencil and scribbled down the address she gave me.

I was about to hang up when she said, "Wait a minute, Tony, Shorty wants to talk to you."

In a moment, Shorty's voice said, "Boss?"

"Yes?"

"I fixed the machine at Big Sam's."

"That's good."

"I thought you'd want to know."

"I knew you'd take care of it." I said. I knew that Shorty needed a little pat on the back so I asked him, "Was it a tough job?"

"Naw," he said, "nothing to it. There was a key caught in the coin slot. Somebody must have run out of nickels."

"What kind of a key?"

"Just a small one."

"What did you do with it?"

"I put it in the museum," Shorty said. Shorty's museum was a collection of slugs, bent and mutilated coins, bits of string and pieces of wire, keys, pieces of metal all fished out of our machines.

"Shorty, I want you to find out what kind of lock that key fits."

"Leave it to me, Boss. Nothing to it."

I hung up and headed for the shower. Now I had something to work on. A blonde and a key. Cookie had been fooling around with the pinball machine. It was quite conceivable he dropped the key in the slot. If he did, he did because he knew I would eventually get it and he wanted me to have it. But why? The answer to that would have to wait until I found out what it unlocked.

I finished my shower and was drying myself when I heard a knock on the door. I finished drying, wrapped the towel around my middle and went to the door. I couldn't figure out who my caller could be. I wasn't expecting anyone.

"Who is it?" I said before opening the door.

"Special delivery," a voice came back.

"Slip it under the door."

"Can't, you have to sign for it."

There was something in the voice that rang a warning bell in my head. I opened the door a crack and looked into the gaping muzzle of a forty-five. The punk that held it had a sneer on his face and a buttermilk complexion, with little chunks of the butter still in it.

"Are you gonna invite me in, little man?"

"Sure, punk," I said, "come on in." I opened the door wide enough for him to enter. When he got about halfway in I slammed the door on him. Hard. Before he could regain his balance I knocked the gun out of his hand and then gave him a vicious judo chop on the side of his neck. As he was going down I brought up my left and felt his nose give way under the impact and then I brought my right up from the floor. That one caught him flush on the mouth. He grovelled on the floor alternately groaning, retching and spitting blood and teeth. I picked up his gun and put him out of his misery with one well placed clout behind the ear.

I went to the phone, dialed police headquarters and asked for Mac. When he answered, I said, "Mac. Tony. Send somebody up to my apartment. I've got a mess here I want you to clean up."

Mac's voice grew tense. "What is it, Tony?"

"Some green punk."

"What was he after?"

"I don't know. I didn't give him a chance to say much. I guess I didn't act very hospitable."

"I'll send a squad car right away."

"No hurry," I said. "He's taking a quiet little nap. And make that an ambulance instead of a squad car."

Mac said, "Tony, I was just going to call you."

"What's up?"

"Where were you this morning?"

"Around."

"You'd better level with me."

"As soon as I think it's important to inform the police of every move I make I'll come down and turn myself in. Now, what's this all about?"

"Do you know a Peggy Marshall?"

"You mean the cocktail waitress?" I felt my hand tightening on the receiver. "What about her?"

"She's dead." I cursed under my breath. Mac continued, "I went up to her apartment this morning to question her about last night. When she didn't answer I got the manager to open her door. The place was a mess. Everything was turned inside out. We found her body in the bedroom."

My throat was dry. "How did she get it?"

Mac's answer didn't surprise me. "Her neck was broken."

"Any leads?"

"Nothing definite. I've got the fingerprint crew going over the place now." He paused. "Now do you want to tell me where you were this morning?"

I thought it over for a minute. I knew they were going to find my fingerprints all over the place. Even if they could fix the exact time of death, I had no witnesses to prove where I was when she got it. I knew that Mac would believe my story but Captain Coletti would have enough circumstantial evidence to send me to the gas chamber.

"Mac, you know I didn't do it."

"Yes," he said, "I know that. Is that all you want to tell me?"

"That's all. Just remember, no matter what it looks like, I didn't do it."

I heard Mac sigh and when he spoke there was dejection in his voice. "I was afraid you'd get mixed up in this thing. You just won't listen."

"Cheer up," I said. "It goes along like this for a while and then it gets worse."

I hung up and got into some fresh clothes. In a hurry. I heard the faint whine of a siren in the distance. I had a lot to do and no time to do it. I tore the page out of the notebook with Lorna's address and stuffed it in my pocket. I grabbed the punk's forty-five and stuck it in my belt. I took the stairs two at a time, jumped into my car and barrelled out of there.

When I got about ten blocks away from my apartment, I pulled my car over to the curb and took Lorna's address out of my pocket. I memorized it, tore up the paper and threw it out of the window. I drove the rest of the way very carefully observing all the traffic regulations. I didn't want to be stopped, especially if Coletti had his hooks out for me.

I didn't know how much time I had. I knew it wouldn't take long for the police to identify my fingerprints and when they did they'd come after me. They'd want a few answers that I wasn't prepared to give. I still had a few questions to ask on my own. Two murders had been committed within twelve hours. Angel Face, if he was the murderer, and there was no doubt in my mind, was getting ready to make a move. If Coletti nabbed me and tried to pin the murders on me, it wouldn't matter if he was successful or not. The action would give Angel Face plenty of time to clear out of town.

But why were the murders committed? Obviously, Cookie knew something. But Peggy? Why Peggy? I was convinced she knew nothing. Unless ... of course, that was it! Hadn't her apartment been searched? Turned inside out, as Mac had expressed it. Somebody was looking for something and whoever it was thought that Peggy had it. It must have been something that Cookie could have given her.

The key!

Suddenly the key took on added significance. If it was important enough to kill for, it could bust this thing wide open. I could take the key and my theories to Mac and let him finish the job. If Coletti would let him. But I knew he wouldn't. Mac would catch the guy sooner or later and duly bring him to trial. And then there would be technical legal delays. Maybe the rat would sit in death row delaying execution for ten years with legal gymnastics. It had been done before. It was being done now.

I wanted to wind this thing up clean. An eye for an eye. A neck for a neck.

I pulled up in front of a gray apartment building on Pacific. It wasn't the fashionable part of Pacific but the neighborhood showed signs that the people who lived there cared about where they lived. I found a nameplate on the wall with the careful inscription, Miss Lorna Williams, printed on a card in the slot. Alongside of the name it said, Apt. 3C. I jabbed a couple of buttons of tenants who lived on the second and fourth floors. I preferred to go up unannounced.

I soon had an answering signal on the front door. I pushed it open, went in, and took the elevator to the third floor. I found 3C and rapped on the door.

A moment later I heard that low sexy voice saying, "Who is it?"

"Special delivery," I said. Why change the script.

"Can you slip it under the door?"

"Afraid not. It has to be signed for."

I pulled the forty-five out of my belt. The door opened a crack. I brought my foot up and kicked it all the way open. She stood there, a look of surprise on her face. She was wearing black velveteen toreador pants and a matching black turtle neck sweater. She was even more stunning in daylight than she was under artificial light. The outfit she wore clung so closely to her beautiful body it looked like it had been painted on. As a matter of fact I could still see the brush marks.

She regained her composure quickly. "Mr. Ceaser, what a nice surprise."

"My friends call me Tony. Remember?"

"You don't seem very friendly with that gun in your hand."

I glanced down at the gun. "I once saw a guy get the top of his head blown off by one of these things. Splattered his brains all over the ceiling. He looked just like a jellyfish that had been run over by a diesel truck." I watched her face as I finished talking. She didn't blink an eye, just stood there smiling.

"I'm afraid I owe you an apology for last night."

"That's not all you owe me, honey."

"Won't you come in and give me a chance to repay you?"

I put the gun away and walked into a nicely decorated living room. The furniture was old and the rug was showing wear but everything in the room was clean and neat. A woman's tasteful touch showed in the lampshades, curtains and pictures on the wall. In addition to the front door there were three other doors, two of them partially open. The doorway in front of me and to my right led to the kitchen. The second doorway on the wall to my left led into a bedroom. The first was closed.

"Nice place," I said.

"Thank you. Have a seat and I'll fix you a drink. Bourbon and soda, isn't it?"

"Yes it is and no thank you."

"Is there something else I can get you?"

"As a matter of fact," I said, after a warning grumble from my stomach, "I haven't eaten since yesterday."

"Fine," she said, "I'll fix us some brunch."

I glanced down at my hands. "I'll go wash," I said, and headed for the closed door."

"No, not in there," she said quickly. "In through the bedroom."

"What's in here?" I asked.

"It's another bedroom but I don't use it anymore. I used to share this apartment with another girl. It was a nice arrangement. We got along well and split the expenses but she had to run off and get married and spoil everything. Now, run along and wash up while I go to work in the kitchen."

The anger and hate I felt was slowly draining away. I had forgotten momentarily, that the police were out looking for me and that Lorna was, in some way, responsible.

I went through the bedroom into the bathroom and washed my hands quickly. Then I made a quick search of the bedroom. I had no idea of what I expected to find. Her closet was crammed with clothes, shoes and hatboxes. Then in her dresser drawer I made a startling discovery; a set of moulded foam rubber pads. So, she was putting on a false front!

I walked into the kitchen where the delicious odor of frying bacon filled the air. The table was set and there was sliced melon at the two places.

"Be ready in a minute," Lorna said cheerily. "Sit down and start on the melon."

"This could be very dangerous," I said.

"Why?" she asked, guardedly.

"A guy could get used to this kind of treatment."

"Is that bad?"

"No, it's good, that's the trouble with it."

She put a platter of bacon and scrambled eggs on the table together with a plate of buttered toast and a pot of coffee. She removed her apron and sat down. I ate like a lumberjack while she pecked away at the food daintily. I finished, shoved my plate away and pulled out my pack of cigarettes. I lit up and leaned back. She poured another cup of coffee for me and as I stared down at it I remembered the cup of coffee I had had earlier that morning. Suddenly there was a knot in my stomach and I felt the hate start spreading again, like a slow acting poison.

She must have seen something in my face. "Everything all right, Tony?"

"Yeah," I said, not too pleasantly, "just fine. Now suppose you play canary and start singing."

"Last night?" she said.

"Last night."

"Shall I tell you everything?"

"You'd better."

"I went to a late movie last night and after it was over I didn't feel like coming home. I felt like listening to a little music so I went to Big Sam's."

"You've been there before?"

"Oh, several times. I just adore Cookie's music..." She stopped, suddenly. Maybe it was the thought that she would never hear Cookie play again. Maybe it was something else. She took a sip of coffee and went on.

"You know, a single girl alone in a bar is asking for trouble. Especially if she's as attractive as you are."

"Thank you," she said. "But I've been around long enough to know how to handle most situations. When you made your move last night I thought you were just another fresh one, but, well, frankly, I was attracted to you. Your approach was direct and to the point. You said in a few words what most men take an evening to say. I liked that."

"Well enough to send me on a wild goose chase. Or maybe," my eyes narrowed, "it wasn't so wild."

"You've got to believe me, Tony," she said softly, "I fully intended to meet you."

"Then what took you so long?"

"I didn't want to follow you out. That would look too obvious. So I sat around for a few minutes and finished my drink. Then I went to the powder room to freshen up a bit. When I came out I walked directly out of the bar and started around to the back."

"What stopped you?"

"When I got about halfway down the street I heard a couple of loud explosions. I got frightened and ran back to Columbus. I walked down to the next corner, caught a cab and came home.

This morning I read what happened in the paper. Oh, Tony, why did it happen?"

"That's what I'm trying to find out. Now suppose you tell me everything that happened after I left last night."

"But, Tony, I just told you."

"I don't mean you. What were the others doing?"

"I didn't really pay attention."

"Where was Big Sam all this time?"

"Behind the bar."

"And Peggy?"

"Peggy? Oh, you mean the cocktail waitress? I believe she left."

"Before you went to the powder room, or after?"

"I think it was—I really don't remember."

"And Cookie, where was he all the time and what was he doing?"

"He didn't do anything. I think he was playing the pinball machine."

"He didn't move from the pinball machine all the time you were there?"

She frowned in concentration. "No—o—wait a minute—yes, he did. I remember now. Just as I was going to the powder room the phone rang. Sam answered the phone behind the bar and then told Cookie to take the call on the other phone."

"The phone next to the ladies room?"

"Yes."

"Could you hear any of the conversation?"

"Yes, I could hear Cookie's voice through the wall. It isn't a very thick partition."

"What was he saying?"

"I don't know. I wasn't paying attention. I just heard the sound of his voice but none of his conversation."

"How long did he talk."

"I don't know. Is all this important?"

"It might be," I said, "when I get all the pieces and then start putting them together. Did he talk as short as a minute or as long as five minutes?"

"No, I think it might have been two or three minutes."

"Think carefully, now," I said. "Two or three minutes can be an awful long time if you're hanging by your thumbs or it can be no time at all if you're engaged in some other more favorable pastime."

"I'd say it was two or three minutes."

"Then what happened?"

"I finished my business in the powder room and walked out."

I paused before my next question never allowing my eyes to leave her face. "Where was Cookie?"

"When?"

"When you left the powder room."

"I—I don't know."

"Was he still on the phone?"

"No, I don't think so."

"Was he back in the bar room?"

"He might have been, although I didn't notice. I just walked straight out."

"Is there any coffee left?"

She lifted the pot. "Yes," she said, "but it might have cooled. Shall I heat it a little?"

"No, don't bother."

She poured some of the dark liquid into my cup and a little into her own. "Have I been of any help, Tony?"

"Depends."

"It depends on what?"

"On whether or not you're telling me the truth."

"But why should I lie to you?"

"I don't know. Why should somebody clip me on the noggin and try to frame me for a murder? Two of them now."

"Two?" she asked, startled. "Who was the other?"

"Peggy."

"The cocktail waitress?"

I nodded my head. She put her head in her hands and sat there silently. "The police think I did it," I said finally.

"You?" She looked at me.

"I was over there this morning. Her place is lousy with my fingerprints. After what happened last night I'm the prime number one suspect. I imagine the police are looking for me right now."

"Oh, Tony, what are you going to do?"

"I don't have much choice," I said grimly. "I've got to find the real killer before the police find me."

"And if you don't?"

I shrugged my shoulders. "I have to. I can't stand the smell of cyanide, it makes me sick to my stomach."

Lorna got up and cleared away the dishes. She washed them and then placed them in a rack to dry. It gave me an opportunity to go over her story in my mind. I still had to get Big Sam's version of what had happened last night and I still needed a lot of answers to questions I hadn't even thought up.

Lorna finished cleaning up and suggested we go back into the living room. After we were seated I said, "It takes a little money to keep up a place like this. Are you independently wealthy?"

"Heavens, no," she laughed. "I'm just a poor working girl."

"Is that right? Where do you work?"

"In a stuffy office on Montgomery."

"How come you're not working today?"

"I'm playing hooky," she said after a brief pause.

"What about your background?"

"What about it?"

"Any family?"

"My folks are dead. I have a brother."

"Where is he now?"

"The last letter I got from him was postmarked 'Nebraska.' " She was silent a moment. "My, you're certainly putting me through the third degree," she said.

"Listen, baby," I said, "I'm playing a game for high stakes— my neck—and when my neck is involved I don't fool around."

"But why take it out on me?" she asked.

"Because," I said, "if it wasn't for you I wouldn't be involved in this thing in the first place."

"Then you think that I had something to do with it?"

"I didn't say that. It's just that I like to keep an open mind. I don't believe anything anybody tells me until I find out for myself that it's the truth."

"That's the second time you've said that."

"Said what?"

"Inferred that I wasn't telling you the truth."

"You want it straight?" I asked her.

"I think I'm entitled to have it straight."

"All right. In my experience with women I've found that if a woman will deceive you in one way, she'll just as easily deceive you in another."

"What are you talking about?"

"I told you I'm playing a game for high stakes. When I went in to wash my hands I took the opportunity to make a fast search of your room."

Her eyes grew cold. "And what did you find?" she asked, tensely.

"I found a set of falsies," I said, bluntly.

She looked startled for a moment and then burst out laughing. "But those don't belong to me," she said. "My ex-roommate, the one I told you about ... "

"Yeah, yeah." I said getting to my feet. "Well, I have to get going."

She stood up and faced me. "You don't believe me," she said. I didn't answer her. "You want me to prove it?" she said in a steady voice. Before I could answer she started pulling her sweater up over her head. She took it off and threw it on the couch. She reached around behind her and unfastened the catches on her brassiere. She hesitated a moment and then lowered it, slowly, until it was off, completely. She let it drop to the floor.

I have seen a lot of bare bosoms in my day. I've seen them in the flesh, I've seen photographs and great paintings, but never have I seen anything to compare with what I saw there.

Her skin was like cream; rich heavy dark cream. Her breasts sloped gently and then erupted into magnificent cherry-tinted peaks. They were proud—no—arrogant, as they stood at attention. There wasn't a mark or a blemish on them. They were perfectly beautiful and beautifully perfect.

"Do you believe me now?" she asked in a voice packed with emotion.

I looked directly into her eyes. "I'm sorry I made you do that, but I'm not too sorry."

In the next moment she was in my arms, her head on my shoulder, sobbing, "You've got to believe me, please, Tony, you must."

What does a guy do in a situation like this?

CHAPTER FIVE

I LEFT LORNA'S APARTMENT and went back to my car. I drove around until I spotted an outside telephone booth at a service station. I dialed police headquarters and asked for Mac.

"McGovern speaking," he said laconically.

"Mac, this is Tony."

There was an instant change in his voice. "Tony, where in the hell are you."

"I'm calling you from a phone booth so don't bother tracing the call."

"Tony," he pleaded, "you've got to turn yourself in."

"What for?" I asked innocently.

"You know damn well what for. Your fingerprints were plastered all over Peggy Marshall's apartment."

"Well, that doesn't mean anything," I said. "It proves I was there but it doesn't prove I killed her."

"It places you at the scene of the death at the approximate time of the death. What does that add up to?" he asked.

"It adds up to a neat frame up," I said, "and I'm in no mood for playing patsy."

"Tony" he said, with an edge of desperation in his voice, "there's a pick-up out on you. Coletti wants you and he doesn't care how he gets you. He means business. Now will you turn yourself in before you get hurt? Better yet, tell me where you are and I'll come down personally and get you."

"And then what happens?"

"And then, well..." His voice trailed off.

"Sure," I said. "At least I'm glad that we're good enough friends where you don't have to feed me a bunch of crap about the square deal I'll get if I turn myself in. I know better and so do you. This is the chance Coletti has been waiting for. I'll just bet he passed the word along that he wants me dead or alive and that there might be a promotion in it for the guy who brings me in feet first.

"Now what about the punk who was in my apartment?"

"We couldn't hold him," Mac said.

"What do you mean, you couldn't hold him?" I demanded. "He busted into my apartment, threatened me with a gun."

"I didn't see you come around pressing charges."

"What for?" I said. "Couldn't you book him on an open charge? Couldn't you hold him without booking him and work him over? Hell, I shouldn't have to tell you your business."

"You don't," Mac said, "but the next time you work a guy over, go easy. We had to send him to a hospital and by the time they had him patched up he had a lawyer there. His story was that he made a business call to your apartment and that you beat him up without any provocation. And that isn't all."

"It's enough," I said.

"No, it isn't," Mac said. "He's pressing charges against you for assault and battery."

"He's a piker," I said, "everybody else wants me for murder."

"This is no joke, Tony."

"You don't hear me laughing do you? Listen, Mac," I said earnestly, "can you call off your dogs for twenty-four hours? If you can I think I can crack this thing."

"Not a chance," Mac said, "you know that. Besides, it's out of my hands anyway."

"Yeah," I said, "I guess I'll just have to do it the hard way."

"How's that?"

"A four and a three," I said, "if I don't crap out first," and I was about to hang up when a thought struck me. "Mac, you said the punk had a lawyer. What was his name?"

"S. H. Bertram," came the reply.

I whistled. "That punk is batting in the big league. Isn't Bertram the mouthpiece that defended Angel Face Lawrence?"

"One and the same," said Mac.

"See you in court," I said and hung up.

I grabbed the phone book and looked up Bertram's office address. It was in the Gross building on Bush street, a couple of blocks away from the Union Square garage. I dialed my office.

"Ceaser Amusement Company."

"Wanda, this is Tony."

"Oh, Tony," she said, "I'm so glad you called instead of coming in. There are two men in a parked car across the street."

"That figures," I said. "What do they look like, cops or robbers?"

"Shorty got a look at their license plate. It's an official car."

"Where is Shorty?" I asked.

"Right here."

"Good. Now, listen carefully. I want you to call the Musician's union and get Cookie's home address. You may have to think up a story. I'll leave that up to you, but get it. Write it down and give it to Shorty. Can the cops see what you're doing?"

"Yes."

"Good. In about fifteen minutes pick up the phone as though you were answering a call. Nod your head a few times, hang up, grab your coat and dash out of there. Jump in your car and hightail it to the Union Square garage."

"Shall I try to lose the cops if they follow me?"

"Hell no," I said, "that's the idea. When you get to Union Square park your car and then go on a leisurely shopping expedition. There's where you can lose the cops if they're still following you. After you've ditched them, go to the cigar stand in the Gross building and ask for an envelope with your name on it. In it, you'll find my parking ticket. Go back to the garage, get my car and drive it to the alley behind Big Sam's. Lock the car and leave the keys on top of the left front tire. Have you got all that?"

"Got it," she said.

"Good, now let me talk to Shorty."

"What's up, boss?" asked Shorty a moment later.

"In about fifteen minutes Wanda is going to lead those cops on a wild goose chase. As soon as they leave you get in the pickup and get out of there. Bring all your keys and your tools. In exactly half an hour from now pick me up in front of the Gross building on Bush street. Be sure you bring the address that Wanda is going to get and bring the key you found in the pinball machine at Big Sam's."

We synchronized our watches and hung up. I got in my car and started driving toward the Union Square garage. I felt that it was more than coincidence that Angel Face Lawrence's attorney should pop into the picture suddenly. Especially representing that two-for-a-nickel hood who had looked to me like he couldn't afford a cup of coffee, much less some of the highest priced legal talent in the city.

I thought back to Angel Face's trial trying to recall some of the highlights. The case had attracted a lot of attention at the time. The local papers were full of it every day. Everybody followed it and everybody discussed it. Bertram had maintained that his client was the victim of a case of mistaken identity and circumstantial evidence. He put on quite a show and the local betting was even money that he would get Lawrence off.

I pulled into the Union Square garage where one of the attendants tore a ticket in half, putting one half under my windshield wiper and giving me the other half. I took my ticket and put it in my breast pocket together with my handkerchief. I walked over to Bush street keeping my eyes open for a novelty store. I found one, went in and bought a Junior G-Man Badge after explaining to the clerk that I wanted it for my young son. While he was busy making change I pinned the badge to my wallet.

From there I walked to the Gross building, found Bertram's name on the register and took the elevator up to his office. So far my luck hadn't been too smashing. I was going to need a couple of breaks to pull this off. I got break number one when I found his outer office empty except for his attractive receptionist. I was glad she was so pretty for this meant Bertram wanted window dressing more than efficiency in his outer office.

She smiled up at me. "Can I help you?"

I put my hands on her desk and looked into her eyes and then down at the top of her scoop necked sweater that didn't do too much to hide the upper part of a well developed bosom. She just sat there smiling up at me so I took the opportunity to notice that her desk held an intercommunication system and a telephone. The telephone was one of those with the glass buttons in the base that allowed two or three calls to come in on one line.

"I'd like to see Mr. Bertram," I said smiling back at her.

"Do you have an appointment?" she asked thumbing through her appointment book.

"No," I said, "but I don't need one." I pulled my wallet out, flashed the badge and quickly put it away. Her eyes grew large and she seemed a bit frightened. Her reaction was perfect. I leaned over the desk and grew very confidential. I put my finger to my lips and whispered, "Not a word of this to anybody." I walked around the desk and into Bertram's private office.

He was seated behind his desk intently studying some documents. He was a man of medium build with no distinguishing characteristics except for the horn rimmed glasses. He looked up when I closed the door and said, "Yes?"

"How do you do, Mr. Bertram," I said civilly. "My name is Tony Ceaser."

He froze for a moment and then his hand darted out toward the telephone.

"I wouldn't do that if I were you," I said unbuttoning my coat so that the forty-five was in plain view.

"What do you want, Mr. Ceasar?" he asked.

"Some information," I said.

"What sort of information?"

"For instance," I said watching his face carefully, "I'd like to know how come a lawyer of your stature is representing a punk like pimple face."

"I have all manner of clients," he answered.

"Who's putting up the money?"

"I'm afraid that's none of your business."

"Come off of it," I said, "you know damn well your client would never show up in court to press that assault and battery charge."

"I don't think that will become necessary," he said. "It is exceedingly difficult to prosecute a man for assault and battery when he is in San Quentin awaiting execution for murder."

I laughed. "They have to catch me first, don't they?"

"They will," he said grimly. "We have a very efficient police department in San Francisco."

"Oh, I don't know," I said casually. "They haven't done a very good job on Angel Face Lawrence."

"Mr. Lawrence, for your information, is innocent of all the charges brought against him."

"That isn't what the jury said."

"He was convicted on circumstantial evidence and on the testimony of unreliable witnesses."

"Save it for the judge," I said. "Tell me, what kind of a position does it put you in communicating with a man wanted by the police and not informing them."

"I fully intend informing them," he said, his eyes narrowing, "as soon as you leave."

"You know damn well I don't mean me."

"If you are referring to Mr. Lawrence, you are assuming a fact that is not in evidence."

"Do you mean to tell me that you haven't been in touch with Lawrence?"

"I don't mean to tell you anything," he said with an air of finality.

"Suppose I told you that I could furnish proof that you have been in contact with Angel Face Lawrence since his escape?"

Bertram gave me a dry laugh. "You're bluffing, Mr. Ceaser, and I don't bluff easily. Besides, even if you could furnish that nebulous proof, of what would it avail you?"

"I don't know much about law, but I do know that as an attorney you are an officer of the court."

"That is correct."

"And as an officer of the court," I continued, "it is your duty to carry out the judgment of the court. If the court judged that Lawrence was guilty and should be sent to San Quentin, isn't it your duty to turn him in?"

"Did you ever study law, Mr. Ceaser?"

"I started to, once."

"What a shame you didn't finish," he said. "If you did, then maybe you wouldn't be wasting my time or yours. Now let me clarify a few things for you. You are assuming that I have been in touch with Mr. Lawrence or vice versa. And assuming that this was true, have you never heard of a privileged communication? Let's carry this one step further. Supposing that you could prove unquestionably that Mr. Lawrence and myself have been conversant? Then what? Can you prove I have broken any law? I haven't aided him in unlawful flight nor have I harbored him.

"If it was your intention to come in here and browbeat me or intimidate me, I am afraid you have failed miserably. The only reason I have tolerated you is because you threatened me with a gun but even that doesn't frighten me. I know you wouldn't dare use it in a crowded building such as this. You wouldn't get to the ground floor before being apprehended." He finished his dissertation and sat back smugly, folding his hands across his middle.

"If you're through," I began, "then I want to tell you a few things. I didn't go to law school because I didn't have the money.

You know what money is, don't you? That's what you get great big gobs of for defending these slimy rats who come crawling to you when they get in a jam. The tougher the jam, the better you like it because then you can pounce on them like a weasel and suck out all their blood." I watched his face closely and saw the color come into his pallid cheeks.

"You don't have a plush office in this fancy building," I continued, "by taking on charity cases. But Angel Face Lawrence was a poor man. He didn't have the kind of money to hire you. As I recall, at the trial you went to great pains to prove how impecunious your client was."

"I take on many cases in the cause of justice," he began.

"Horseshit!" I said. "You took him on because you knew he had half a million bucks stashed away somewhere and you couldn't wait to get your grubby hands on it. But you were in for a disappointment when you found out that money was hot. So for the last two years you've been sitting in your cozy little office trying to figure out a way to unload it. And here's where I give the devil his due; you figured out a scheme to do it. But there was just one hitch—at the last minute the loot disappeared. And you want to know something?"

He took off his glasses and wiped them nervously as he squinted up at me. He was a smart cookie. He had let me know in no uncertain terms that he couldn't be bluffed. Now, by his silence, he was letting me know that I had guessed what had been going on. I leaned over his desk and pulled the handkerchief out of my breast pocket to wipe my forehead. As I did so, my parking ticket fell onto his desk. I scooped it up quickly and put it back into my pocket, but not before he had a chance to see it.

"You want to know something?" I repeated, very slowly, very softly. "I know where that money is."

I turned around, walked out of his office and closed the door behind me gently. As soon as I did, I whipped over to the receptionist and told her to give me an envelope. I scribbled Wanda's name on it, put the parking ticket in it and handed it to the girl. I hoped she was still impressed by the phony badge.

"Quick," I said, "take this down to the cigar counter and leave it there. Tell them that the woman whose name is on the envelope will pick it up soon."

She started to object but I grabbed her arm and gave her a start to the door. "Official business," I said patting my wallet, "no time to lose. Now hurry."

As soon as she was gone I got behind her desk. I saw that one of the buttons on the telephone was lit indicating that Bertram was placing a call. I pressed the button down and lifted the receiver gently. I heard the distant ringing. Soon a voice answered.

"Get me Mr. Yee, quickly," said Bertram.

There was a brief pause and then another voice came on the phone. "Yee speaking."

"Charlie, this is Bertram. Tony Ceaser was just here."

"Good," said the voice belonging to Charlie. "Call the police and have him picked up. He can't be too far away."

"I'm afraid I can't do that."

"Why?"

"I think he knows the whereabouts of a certain package."

"Oh, so," said Charlie, "then we had better find him before the police do. Where is he now?"

"I, very astutely, found out he parked his car in the Union Square garage," said Bertram. "Get some men over there right away."

I eased the receiver back onto the cradle and walked out of the office. I glanced at my watch. Shorty was due to pick me up in two minutes. The timing was perfect.

I pushed the button for the elevator and waited. When the elevator arrived, Bertram's receptionist stepped out. I grabbed her arm and whispered into her ear, "Not a word about this to anybody. Not even him," I said inclining my head toward the office. "J. Edgar wouldn't like it."

I took the elevator to the ground floor and walked out onto the street. Shorty pulled up, I jumped into the pickup and said, "Get going, fast."

"Where to, boss?"

"Did Wanda give you Cookie's address?" He nodded. "That's where we're going."

I could see that Shorty was bursting with questions and several times started to say something but he evidently thought better of it and remained silent. That was one of the things I admired about Shorty. He knew when to keep his mouth shut.

I was grateful for Shorty's silence for it gave me a chance to think. Now a new character had entered our little play; Charlie Yee. Who was he and how did he fit in? The name sounded oriental but the voice sounded occidental, with the trace of a British accent. It could be possible that he was Eurasian or he could be Chinese with a western education. He could have come from Hong Kong and attended an English school there. But what was his connection with the case?

Charlie Yee, Charlie Yee. I repeated it to myself several times. It had a familiar ring and yet I couldn't place it.

Shorty reached into his pocket, extracted a key and handed it to me. "What's this?" I asked.

"It's the key I found in the pinball machine. You said you wanted it."

I had forgotten all about it. I examined it closely. There was a number 12 stamped on it. "Did you find out what kind of lock it fits?"

Shorty nodded his head. "It's a key to a locker of some sort. You see, there's the name of the manufacturer embossed on one side?"

I turned the key over and looked at it. There was writing on it but it was so small I couldn't make it out. "What about it?"

"I checked that manufacturer's catalogue and found out they are the company that makes those lockers you find in the bus stations and train depots."

"Shorty, I could kiss you."

He grinned. "You do and I'll turn you in to the cops myself." Then he sobered immediately. "Boss, it looks awful bad for you. Have you seen the papers?" I shook my head. "Boy," he said, "some of them are sure riding Coletti's tail."

"How come?" I asked.

"They say that Coletti had you locked up once when they caught you dead to rights with a body but he released you because of insufficient evidence. Then they find another body, killed the same way and your fingerprints all over the victim's apartment."

"What has Coletti said to all this?"

"He's putting the blame on McGovern."

I sat up straight. "What?"

"Well, maybe not in so many words—you know they can't show any signs of disagreement on the force—but he's hinting that McGovern released you against Coletti's better judgment. And the papers are hinting that you and McGovern are pretty good buddies. All in all, it doesn't look too good for McGovern."

I swore under my breath. It was bad enough for me to be stuck in the mire without dragging Mac through it. If this case didn't crack wide open—and soon—Mac would get it in the neck. He would be forced into resigning and that would kill him. For a brief moment I considered turning myself in or, better yet, letting Mac bring me in. But that would solve nothing. It might appease Coletti and the newspapers but look what happened when Chamberlin appeased Hitler.

We rode the rest of the way to Cookie's apartment in silence. Sharp little teeth of frustration began to gnaw around the edges of my subconscious mind. What had started out as a simple manhunt had now evolved into a complex drama with more characters introduced at frequent intervals. But where was Angel Face? Bertram had said that the San Francisco police department wasn't stupid and he was right. But why hadn't they turned up anything on Angel Face for the last two years? If he was living in the city how could he be so completely swallowed up as to leave no trace? If he was living—the phrase came back into my mind. "What if he wasn't living?" What if he was eliminated by some person or persons who wanted to get that half a million in cold hard cash? But if he wasn't living why was someone so anxious to frame me for a couple of murders that had Angel Face's signature written all over them?

CHAPTER SIX

I HAD SHORTY STOP the pickup a couple of blocks away from Cookie's apartment. I didn't want to take any unnecessary chances in case the place was being watched. I told Shorty to bring his keys and whatever tools might be necessary to help us force our way into the apartment. We walked the two blocks casually, as though we were a couple of lugs who had a day off and had nothing to do. We couldn't afford to attract any attention to ourselves.

We found the apartment house and walked up to the front door. While I checked the cards to determine Cookie's apartment number, Shorty brought out his huge key ring and started working on the door. In a few seconds he had it open. We walked in and up to Cookie's apartment. So far we had been fortunate for we had encountered no one. Shorty again brought his keys out, fiddled around, and opened the door.

"Okay, Shorty," I said, "you go on back and wait for me in the pickup. If I'm not there in fifteen minutes, beat it."

"How come?" he wanted to know.

"There's no use of you getting involved in this thing any more than you are already."

"What kind of a guy do you think I am?" he asked indignantly. "If you get into any trouble you'll need my help to get out."

I grinned. It was exactly the kind of answer I expected. "Now be careful," I said, "we don't want to leave our fingerprints around the place. I'm sure the police have been here already, but they may come back."

We started looking around the apartment. It was a tiny place, just the one room that served as living room and bedroom and a kitchenette that was no bigger than a good sized closet. There was a divan that made up into a bed flanked by a couple of wrought iron end tables. There was a homemade bookcase against one wall, consisting of a couple of glass building blocks supporting a shelf. There were a couple of chairs, a table, a hi-fi set and records, and little else in the room. We went over everything carefully.

"I guess we've drawn a blank," I said after a while.

Shorty didn't answer me. He was busy going through a small closet that nestled in the corner of the room. I walked over to watch him. He was busily going through the pockets of all the garments hanging there. So far his search had produced a comb, a handkerchief, the stub of a theatre ticket and a program of the San Francisco Civic Light Opera Association. "That's all I can find," he said finally.

I examined the objects and was about to hand them back to Shorty when I noticed something on the Opera program. It was one of those programs that contained advertising as well as information. One of the ads was for the Lambertson Travel Bureau on Post street. Some of the copy read, "Let us plan your itinerary. We make the arrangements, you have the fun. South American tours our specialty." The reason the ad caught my attention was because I noticed that the program had been folded and refolded several times and the edges of the creases were dirty. When I folded it along the creased edges, the travel bureau ad stood out prominently.

I handed the things back to Shorty to put away and motioned for him to follow me out. We walked down the hallway toward the stairs but we stopped when we heard voices drifting up.

"So I seen these two guys coming up the stairs to the front door. I knew they were strangers in the neighborhood but I thought they were salesmen. We get lots of door to door salesmen in this neighborhood. But when they didn't ring my bell, I got suspicious. And then when I saw one of them fiddling with the lock on the front door I called the police."

"And you say they're still up there?" said the other voice.

"Yup," said the first voice. "I been watching for them and I know they haven't come down."

"Is there any other way out besides these stairs?"

"Well, there's some wooden stairs on the outside of the apartments that are supposed to be used as a fire escape but nobody ever uses them. Besides, I would have seen them come down because those stairs go right by my kitchen window."

"I'll go out and tell my partner to watch the back stairs and then we'll go up."

We heard the sound of a door opening as I motioned to Shorty to follow me back to Cookie's room. Shorty got his keys out but had trouble finding the right key. After what seemed like a period of ten years, he got the door open and we went in. I grabbed a chair and propped it up under the door knob and then hooked up the chain on the night latch.

"What do we do now?" Shorty whispered. "We're trapped."

"Desperate times call for desperate measures," I whispered back. "Go into the kitchenette and ease the back door open. Peek out and see if you can see the other cop down below. If you can, give me a whistle, then stay there and keep him in sight."

Shorty nodded and headed for the kitchenette. I waited and soon heard a low whistle. I pulled the forty-five out and released the safety catch. I heard footsteps out in the hallway and then the sound of a key being fitted into the lock. I heard the key turning slowly and then I waited until I saw the knob begin to turn. I took careful aim and put two slugs high up on the door. I heard sounds of confusion on the other side of the door and then another whistle from Shorty. I headed for the kitchenette.

"He's gone," Shorty whispered excitedly. "As soon as he heard the shots he tore out of there."

"Let's go," I said and led the way down the back stairs. My only hope was that the other cop had headed up the front stairs to help his partner when he heard the shots. If he went to the car to radio for more help, we were through. But even if he did go running upstairs we weren't out of the woods. Our pickup was two blocks away.

We reached the bottom of the stairway and edged around to the corner of the building. The patrol car was parked out in front and there was no one in sight.

"Come on," I said to Shorty and we ran to the patrol car. I slid in under the steering wheel and had the car started by the time Shorty had clambered into the other side. I went screeching around the corner and headed back toward where the pickup was parked. I stopped around the corner from where it was parked and told Shorty to walk over to it. If no one saw him get out of the patrol car and into the pickup, it would be impossible to tie him in with this caper.

"But what about you?" Shorty asked before he slammed the door.

"Never mind me," I said, "head back to the store and stay there." I knew I had to ditch the car in a hurry because it wouldn't be long before every police car in the city would be looking for it. A minute later the call came over the radio.

I drove around for a few minutes keeping to the back streets until I spotted a narrow alley. I pulled into the alley, parked the car and beat it out of there. I walked up three blocks until I came to a main thoroughfare. I saw a squad car go screaming by followed, a few minutes later, by another one.

I flagged a taxi, climbed in and told him to take me to the Sheraton-Palace Hotel. When we got there I walked in through the front door, sauntered leisurely through the lobby and then out the side door. I got into another taxi and told him to take me to the Lambertson Travel Bureau on Post street. I settled back, lit up a cigarette and relaxed.

The Lambertson Travel Bureau was a small place. It had a cluttered up look for every available inch of wall space was taken up by colorful posters and signs extolling the virtues of everything from Airlines to Zebras. There was a counter that ran the length of the room and it was heaped high with brochures and pamphlets. A thin, fidgety clerk stood behind the counter talking to a middle aged couple.

I moved down to the opposite end of the counter and casually leafed through some pamphlets.

"This is our first vacation in twenty-eight years," I heard the man say.

The clerk forced a smile. "Isn't that nice? Well, I'm sure that we can—"

"And we want it to be a good one," interrupted the man. "Isn't that right, Mama?"

"That's right, Papa," said Mama.

"Yes, well," began the clerk.

"But we don't want to spend too much money," warned the man. "Not with the price of eggs being what it is."

"Eggs?" asked the clerk, a bit bewildered.

"We're in the chicken business," explained the man, "in Petaluma."

"Oh," said the clerk without enthusiasm and to no one in particular. "Now about this trip—"

"Do you eat eggs?" demanded the man suddenly.

The clerk became flustered. "Well I, that is, I—"

"You do or you don't?" insisted the man.

"Yes, yes, of course I do," said the clerk.

"Every day?"

"Well, maybe not every day. Some mornings I like a bowl of cereal."

"You should eat them every day," said the man. "They're good for you and they're high in protein."

"I will, I will," the clerk almost screamed. "And now about this trip. I'd like to suggest—"

"I tell you what," said the man, "we'll think it over. Won't we Mama? After all, the first time in twenty-eight years."

"Almost twenty-nine," said Mama, as they turned around, locked arms and walked out.

The clerk rolled his eyes upward, clenched his fists and started muttering under his breath. "Eggs," he said, and moved down the counter toward me. He composed his features and managed to force his smile again.

"Planning a trip, sir?" he asked.

"Yes," I said, "but not for myself, for a friend of mine."

"Oh," he said, "and where would you like to send him?"

"To San Quentin," I said and before he was able to overcome his surprise, I whipped out my wallet, let him take a fast glance at the phony badge and then put it away quickly.

He gulped several times and then managed to say, "What is it you want?"

"I'm checking up on a possible client of yours. His name is Jacques Coquette. His nickname was Cookie. About your build, maybe a little shorter."

"Yes, yes, I seem to recall the gentleman. I believe I was planning a trip for him. As a matter of fact, he was in several times."

"Where was he planning to go?"

"Let me see," said the clerk, knitting his brow. "We have so many people planning trips. Let me check the files." He went over to a filing cabinet and began thumbing through some cards. He stopped after a moment, frowned and tilted his head. He came back over to where I was standing.

"As I recall," he said, "our planning didn't advance as far as setting up an itinerary. "Yes," he said nodding his head, "now I remember. He wanted some information about South America. That's our specialty, you know."

"What sort of information?"

"Oh, just general information."

"Did he mention any specific country or any specific date?"

"No," said the clerk, "I don't believe so."

"When he came in, was he alone?"

"I believe he was."

"When was the last time he was in?"

"I think just a couple of days ago, although I can't be certain. We do get so many people—"

"From Petaluma and all over," I said. "Now can you think of anything else he said, did or indicated?"

He thought, shook his head and said, "No, I can't think of a thing except but—no, that couldn't be important."

"What couldn't be important?" I demanded.

"Oh, it's really nothing. Not even unusual. Lots of people do the same thing. I don't even know why I thought of it."

"Would you mind telling me what?"

"Not at all," he said politely. "You see, when most people plan a trip they like to know exactly how much it's going to cost them. That's why they use a service such as ours. We can give them exact figures on transportation, hotel accommodations, meals, in fact, everything. And if there's a way to save money, we'll know about it."

"I'm sure you will," I said, "but what are you driving at?"

"Like I said, we like to plan the whole trip. We work on commission, you know, so the more the trip costs, the more we make. Now, this gentleman you're referring to, he wanted to know all about the different means of transportation to these various cities and times and dates of departure, but he never once mentioned the return trip."

"Is that so unusual?" I said.

"When people go someplace, they usually come back," he said.

"Not necessarily," I said. "As a matter of fact, your client just went on a one way trip."

"He didn't," said the clerk, "and after all the time I spent with him. Who is he doing business with now?"

"The morgue," I said and I turned around and walked out.

CHAPTER SEVEN

I STOOD OUT ON THE STREET and noticed that the shadows had begun to lengthen. I glanced at my watch. It was getting late in the afternoon. I intended to see Big Sam before he went to work but I still had a little time to kill. I glanced down the sidewalk which was beginning to fill up with people getting off work. Then I noticed something that made my heart beat a little faster. It was a familiar head of golden hair.

I walked rapidly toward the figure that was by now losing itself in the crowd. I broke into a run and caught up to her at the end of the block.

"Lorna, what are you doing here?"

She stopped short and slowly turned. She looked at me for a moment and then said, "Hello."

I waited a moment. "Is that all you've got to say?"

She smiled. "What do you want me to say?"

"Listen," I said, "I've got a little time to kill and I feel like talking. Let's pop into a quiet little bar and have a drink." I took her arm and started leading her up the street.

"Wait a minute," she said, "I've got a few things to do. Can I meet you somewhere later?"

"Are you trying to get rid of me?"

"No, no," she said, "it's just that—I'm supposed to meet someone and I'm afraid I'm a bit late."

"Oh, it's like that," I said.

"No, it isn't a bit like that. Can't I meet you somewhere later? You name it, I'll be there."

"Okay," I said. "Make it Paoli's at seven. I'll meet you at the bar."

"It's a date," she said and was gone.

I stood there watching her disappear into the crowd. I couldn't understand the apparent change that had come over her since our last meeting. When I had left her apartment she had been warm and outgoing. Now she had seemed cold and distant. I shrugged my shoulders. Women, I thought, who can figure them out? But there was something else nagging me. It wasn't only her attitude that seemed different, but her appearance as well. Of course, that's it, I thought, she was dressed differently.

I hailed a passing taxi and climbed in.

"Where to?" asked the cabbie.

"Just drive around," I said, "I have some thinking to do."

"Listen, buddy," said the cabbie, "this is the rush hour for me. Why don't you let me drop you off at a nice quiet bar where you can do your thinking and I can pick up a few more fares."

"What's the matter?" I said. "Afraid I won't pay you. Do I look like a bum or something?"

"Now, don't get me wrong," he said, "your money's as good as the next guy's."

"Then what's eating you?"

"It's just that while I'm ferrying you to nowhere I could be picking up a half a dozen short hops and long tips."

"So that's what eating you," I said. I pulled a five dollar bill off my roll and threw it into the front seat. "Be a good boy and there may be another one just like it."

"Yes sir," he said. "Anyplace in particular?"

"No, just drive." I settled back and shut my eyes. Again, I went over the information I had accumulated and tried to fill in the blanks. I thought about Charlie Yee and that silly phrase popped into my mind, "Charlie eel make a deal." Charlie Yee. Charlie eel. Charlie eel. Charlie Yee. What if someone said, "Charlie Yee will make a deal," only they said it real fast and some of the words ran together. It would sound like, "Charlie Yee'll make a deal." It would certainly fit in with what I had learned.

But then I had a disquieting thought. If there was a tie-in between what Peggy had overheard and the murders, then Lorna was right back in the middle of things. I'd find out about that at Paoli's at seven o'clock.

I lit up a cigarette and started humming a little tune, "Charlie Yee'll make a deal, Charlie Yee'll make a deal."

"He sure will," said the cabbie.

"What was that?"

"What was what?" asked the cabbie.

"What you just said?"

"I just said what you said."

"Now, wait a minute. Let's start all over. I said, 'Charlie Yee'll make a deal.' "

"And I said, 'He sure will.' "

"Do you know Charlie Yee?"

"Nope," said the cabbie.

"Then how do you know he'll make a deal?" I asked in exasperation.

"I said I didn't know him but I know of him."

"What do you know about him?"

"He's a wheel over in Chinatown."

"What does he do?" I asked.

"He has an export-import business on Grant Avenue. Has his hands in all kinds of schemes."

"What kind of schemes?"

"Oh, a little of this and little of that."

"What in the hell is a little of this and a little of that?"

"How should I know?" asked the cabbie, shrugging his shoulders. "I'm just telling you what I've picked up here and there."

I peeled another five off of the roll and threw it into the front seat. It came flying right back.

"When I tell you that's all I know, then that's all I know," said the cabbie indignantly.

I laughed and threw the bill back at him. "That's for being honest," I said. "What's your name, anyway?"

"Joe Pinsky, you wanna make something out of it?"

"No," I said, "I just want to be your friend."

"Okay by me," he said reaching back to shake hands, "what's your name?"

I hesitated a moment, then decided to trust him. "Mine's Tony Ceaser," I said clasping his hand. I waited for his reaction. There was none. "Do you know who I am?"

"Naw," he said, "I never read the newspapers."

"That's good," I said.

"And besides," added Joe, "I don't think you're guilty."

I laughed again. "Something tells me that this is the beginning of a beautiful friendship."

"Seems to me you had a beautiful friendship with that cocktail waitress."

"I did," I said. "I was over there this morning. It couldn't have been too long before she was killed."

"How do you figure?"

"When I left her apartment I went directly to my own. I had a drink, made a phone call and took a shower. When I got out of the shower I had a caller, some punk with a forty-five. He wasn't a very smart punk. I took his gun away and gave him a few lumps. Then I called Lt. McGovern to come and get him. That's when McGovern told me that Peggy—that was the cocktail waitress—was dead."

"How did he know?" asked Joe.

"He had just come from there. He wanted to question her about the other murder. He found her in the bedroom with her neck broken and the whole apartment upside down."

"How long do you figure it was from the time you left her apartment until you talked to McGovern?"

I did some mental calculating. "I'd say from forty to forty-five minutes."

"How long do you figure it would take McGovern to go from this Peggy's apartment back to police headquarters?"

"I'd say from ten to fifteen minutes."

"And he must have spent some time going over the apartment for clues," Joe said. "How much time would he normally spend?"

"That's hard to say."

"Would he spend as much as fifteen, twenty minutes?" Joe asked.

"That's very possible."

Joe was silent for a few minutes. "It doesn't look too good for you, Tony."

"I know that," I said. "They found my fingerprints all over the place."

"That's not what I mean," said Joe. "Adding up all the time that it took McGovern to look around her apartment and drive back to police headquarters, that leaves only about five or ten minutes between the time that you left her apartment and McGovern got there."

"I see what you're driving at," I said. "Hardly enough time for someone else to get into her apartment, kill her, ransack the place and get out without being seen leaving by McGovern."

"Don't get me wrong," said Joe. "I still don't think you did it. You don't seem like that kind of a guy. After you've been driving hack as long as I have you get to know a lot about people. I'm just telling you how it's liable to look to the cops."

"You don't have to tell me how it looks to the cops," I said, "I used to be one myself."

"So what's your move now?" asked Joe.

"That's easy," I said. "All I've got to do is find the real killer before the cops find me."

"Are you making any headway?"

"I don't know," I said, "I have several leads and a few theories, but nothing real definite."

"Is Charlie Yee one of your leads?"

"He's tied into the thing somewhere. Only I can't figure where."

"Why don't you go ask him?" Joe said innocently.

"Yeah," I said, "why don't I. Do you know where his place is?"

"We're practically there," Joe said.

I looked out of the window and noticed for the first time that we were driving along Grant Avenue, the narrow cluttered main street of San Francisco's Chinatown. It isn't the kind of street you'd take if you were in a hurry to get somewhere.

"I doubt if I'll be able to find a parking place," Joe said.

"When we get there, you just let me off and then circle around the block. I shouldn't have any trouble but in case I don't come out in fifteen minutes, call McGovern."

"Gotcha," said Joe as he eased the cab to a stop. "This is it."

I climbed out of the cab in front of an unpretentious building with conservative lettering on the large plate glass window. It said, "CHARLES YEE—FINE ART OBJECTS," and below that in smaller letters, "CHARLES YEE EXPORT-IMPORT CO." There were also some Chinese characters printed on the window.

I went inside and immediately noticed the contrast between the gaudy, raucous carnival atmosphere of Grant Avenue and the quiet, sedate refined decor of Charlie Yee's shop. It was cool and dark inside. There were exquisite vases on display together with pieces of hand-hammered silver and ornate ivory carvings.

A small voice to my right said, "May I help you?"

I looked over toward the voice and saw what appeared to be a life-sized figurine of a Chinese doll, only this one was alive.

"I'd like to see Mr. Yee," I said, then added, "on a matter of confidential business."

Without a word she disappeared behind a curtained doorway at the rear of the shop. I busied myself examining the fine art objects. There was nothing cheap in the shop. The lowest price I found was thirty-five dollars for a small hand carved ivory cigarette holder. I started to take a mental inventory, adding the cost of the various items as I went along but I had to give up for want of an adding machine. In a few minutes the doll returned.

"Would you come this way please?" she asked, holding aside the curtain. I followed her through, down a narrow hallway and then into a room at the right. As soon as she saw that I was in the room she turned around and walked out.

The room was illuminated by soft indirect lighting. The walls were covered with oriental tapestries and the floor had a Persian rug on it, so thick that I almost lost my shoes. In one corner there was a teakwood desk but instead of it holding papers, wire baskets and all the assorted paraphernalia you normally associate with an office desk, it was heaped high with fresh fruit.

Behind the desk, calmly munching on a bunch of grapes, sat the biggest hulk of a man I had ever seen. I thought at first that he was bald but later noticed that his head was completely shaved. He looked like a mammoth Buddha, only I've never seen a Buddha eating grapes.

"Forgive me for not rising," he said in a deep resonant voice, "but as you can see from my ample amount of flesh, for me it is not an easy task. Please take a seat and join me in some fruit."

I selected a bamboo chair and sat down. I sniffed the air. "What kind of incense are you burning?" I asked.

"I have it specially imported," he said. "As you can tell from the delightful fragrance of orange blossoms, it is not for peasants or tourists but for the sensitive nostrils of the true connoisseur. Now, what is it that I may have the pleasure of doing for you?"

"First," I said, "let me introduce myself. The name is Ceasar, Tony Ceaser."

He didn't blink an eyelash. He merely popped another grape into his mouth. "My pleasure, Mr. Ceasar."

"I believe I have something that you want."

"And what might that be, Mr. Ceaser?"

"I'll play your silly little game, Mr. Yee. I have a certain package that I have reason to believe you would like to have in your possession."

"There are many packages I would like to have in my possession."

"But there is only one like this one."

"Do you have it with you?"

"What kind of an idiot do I look like?"

He picked up another bunch of grapes and held them to the light. "You look like the kind of idiot," he began, "who reached for a golden rope only to learn he had a tiger by the tail. Now he's afraid to hold on and he's afraid to let go."

"Wrong, Mr. Yee," I said, "I eat tigers for breakfast."

He made a face. "I'm afraid that I would find them rather unpalatable. I am also afraid that I am in no position to do business with you."

"Why not?"

"I have nothing to offer you in return."

"I think you have."

"And what might that be?"

"Tell me where I can find Angel Face Lawrence."

He laughed. It sounded like the rumble from the pit of an erupting volcano. "You want me to produce a man the police have been unable to find for two years?"

"That's right."

"You flatter me. I thank you, sir. But may I ask what you wish of him?"

"You know damn well what I wish of him."

"Temper, temper, Mr. Ceaser," he chided me. "Violence only produces more violence. As for your offer, I shall need a little time to consider it."

"Time is something I don't have much of right now. Either we do business or we don't. Which is it going to be?"

"I am afraid what you ask might take a little doing."

"Then you'd better start doing it," I said. "I don't have to point out to you how profitable it is going to be for you. You get rid of a partner, eliminate the middleman and keep the package all to yourself."

"If you are trying to appeal to the greed in me you are succeeding quite well. However, I am afraid that what you suggest is quite impossible."

"Why?" I asked.

"Frankly, Mr. Ceaser, I don't trust you. Although your offer is tempting, I find it a little too tempting. It is contrary to human nature to trade a fortune for a worthless human life. That is what you propose to do. In addition, I have virtually no assurance that you can either produce or deliver a package of value."

"How's a half a million bucks in cash?" I asked. "Has that got any value?"

"That depends," he said, slowly munching a grape. "If you could produce a half a million dollars in freshly minted currency or a certified check for a half a million dollars or a legitimate bill of sale for a half a million dollars worth of merchandise, then I might say you have something of value. However, if you should have in your possession a half a million in marked or catalogued bills in which certain government agencies have generated an unusual interest then I would say you are at a distinct disadvantage."

"Well, I guess I've come to the wrong place," I said getting to my feet.

"Let us not be too hasty," said Charlie. "After all, this is a delicate matter and, as such, must be handled with infinite care."

I sat down again. "What's your offer?"

"I wasn't aware that I was about to make one just yet. I may devise some way to help you out of your difficulty, but I would hardly say you are in a position to bargain."

"Is that right?" I said. "Just what would you say?"

"I might quote you an old proverb from my country, 'He who rides the tiger finds it difficult to dismount.' "

"That's very interesting," I said, "but I'd like to quote you a proverb from my country."

"Please do," said Charlie halting a grape on the way to his mouth and leaning forward intently. "Proverbs fascinate me. What is yours?"

"Shit or get off the pot," I said.

He stared at me for a moment, his lower jaw hanging open. Then he quickly completed the journey of the grape to his mouth, munched a couple of times and started laughing, a little at a time, like an earthquake in reverse, sending out shock waves first then building into a body shattering tremor that convulsed his several fat acres. "You have a tremendous sense of humor, Mr. Ceaser."

"Yeah," I said, "I'll probably die laughing, only that isn't laughing gas they give you in San Quentin." I got up on my feet again. "If you are through playing cat and mouse, I'll leave. I never could do a very convincing mouse."

"I'm very sorry we had to meet under such difficult circumstances," he said. "And I am afraid that you will tell your friends that I have been a poor host. Won't you at least partake of some of this delicious fruit before you leave?"

"Maybe I will," I said selecting a reddish-blue bunch of Tokay grapes that looked especially juicy. "Are these good?" I asked.

"Ah," he said, "the finest."

"That's swell," I said. I leaned over his desk and mashed the grapes in his face. He sat there with a bewildered look on his face, bits of the pulp and grape skins clinging to his nose and the juice forming droplets on his puffy jowls.

I didn't bother saying good-bye.

CHAPTER EIGHT

W HEN I GOT BACK OUTSIDE I didn't see Joe's cab. I glanced at my watch. I had been gone less than fifteen minutes. I hoped that Joe didn't get cold feet and run to call McGovern. I was beginning to think it was a mistake to trust him when I heard a horn blaring half way down the block. Joe had found a parking place and was letting me know where he was. I trotted down the street and climbed into the cab.

"Any luck?" Joe asked anxiously.

"To quote an old Chinese proverb," I said, " 'The fish never sees the hook, only the bait.' "

"So you set a trap?"

"Not exactly," I said. "You might say I'm just casting around."

"What are you using for bait?"

"My neck."

"How do you figure Charlie Yee is tied into this thing?"

"It's a long story, Joe."

"Go ahead, I've got lots of time."

"Start driving, Joe." He started up and pulled out into the stream of traffic. "How much do you know about this case?"

"Not too much. Piano player got knocked off last night and someone tried to frame you. Then the cocktail waitress from the same joint gets knocked off this morning and you leave your calling cards all over her place. How much more is there?"

"This thing is like an iceberg. All you can see is the tip of it."

"What's it look like underneath?"

"A half a million bucks."

Joe let out a low whistle. "Where does that fit in?"

"The missing loot from that armored car robbery two years ago."

"You mean the one where they're still looking for Angel Face Lawrence?" Joe asked watching my face in the mirror.

I nodded. "The police seem to think that Cookie—that was the piano player's name—got mixed up in the deal somehow and had to be bumped. They don't know what his connection was but I think I do. I think that somehow he got his hands on the money and stashed it away. I don't know what he intended to do with it because that dough is hot—red hot. I think he stashed it in a locker in the bus terminal or train depot and I think this is the key." I held the key in front of his face.

"How did you get the key?"

"I have a pinball route. The place where Cookie worked was one of my stops. I think Cookie dropped it in the coin chute of my machine last night a short time before he was killed."

Joe was spending more time watching the rear view mirror than the street in front of him. "Don't look now but we've got a tail."

"That figures," I said.

"Shall I lose them?"

"No hurry," I said, "I want to get a look at them first." I leaned back and sat in the corner. I sneaked a look out of the back window and caught a glimpse of a dark green sedan. "Can you lose them without them getting wise that we know we're being tailed?"

Joe laughed. "Just watch me."

Instead of speeding up, Joe slowed down. Traffic was heavy and there were three lanes of it in either direction. We were in the middle lane, our tail directly behind us. The green sedan wasn't too close. Whoever was driving it didn't want to tip us off that we were being tailed so he tried to maintain a respectable distance. When Joe slowed down, the green sedan slowed down even more for fear of getting too close. When the gap between the two cars widened enough to permit room for another car, a car on our right darted into the vacancy. Joe pulled over into the right lane and turned at the next corner. The green sedan, wedged in the middle lane had no choice but to continue forward. It was all done so smoothly I marvelled at the simplicity.

"It always works," Joe said. "If you can get enough room between you and the car behind you, it never fails that a car from the left lane or the right lane will try to squeeze in. Don't ask me why. People are nuts, I guess. They figure if there's a gap in a line of traffic that line is moving faster than the one they're in. So it's just like a football play, you can go either to the right or the left."

"Joe," I said, "you're a genius."

"I know it," he said without modesty, "but nobody appreciates me. Where to now?"

"Take me to Big Sam's on Columbus. Know where it is?"

He nodded his head, hunched over the wheel, put his foot on the carburetor and had me there within three minutes.

When we got there I didn't bother looking at the meter. I handed him a twenty dollar bill and told him to keep it.

"Hey, this is way too much," he protested.

"No, it isn't," I said, "that trick you taught me is worth the price by itself."

"Listen, pal, if you ever need me, just give a whistle and I'll be there. When you call the cab company just tell them you want number seven eleven."

"No wonder I've been so lucky," I said. "I won't forget it." We shook hands and he drove off.

I was taking a chance going in to see Big Sam. For all I knew the cops could have had the place staked out. I was gambling on the chance that they wouldn't because it was too obvious.

I had wanted to catch Big Sam before he went to work but I noticed that the time had slipped by rapidly and it was now a few minutes past six. I looked up and down both sides of the street and saw nothing suspicious. I walked to the corner and saw nothing out of the ordinary on the side street. I went back to Big Sam's and cautiously opened the front door.

There were about a half a dozen people at the bar, men in work clothes, who had evidently stopped in for a beer on their way home from work.

Big Sam, as usual, was polishing glasses.

I strolled down to the far end of the bar, which was deserted, and climbed onto a stool. Big Sam sauntered over, started to say something and then did a double take.

"Tony, what are you doing here?"

"I came in for a drink. You're open for business, aren't you?"

"Sure, sure." He poured a bourbon and soda and set it down in front of me.

I tilted my head toward the other end of the bar. "Who are those guys?"

"They're all working stiffs. They usually stop in every night. I know every one of them."

"Have the cops been in?"

"Not since last night or early this morning, whichever way you want to look at it. They could have come in during the day only Tom never said anything."

"Did Tom tell you I was here this morning?"

"No," said Big Sam shaking his head. "It looks like you've got yourself into a jackpot."

"I'm not as bad off as you are," I said.

"What do you mean?"

"You just lost two of your employees. What are you going to do now?"

"I can always get another cocktail waitress, although Peggy was a good girl. Nice personality if you know what I mean. Say," he said suddenly, earnestly, "you didn't really have anything to do with it, did you?"

"I had about as much to do with it as you did."

"It just doesn't make any sense," said Big Sam slowly. "Why, Tony, can you tell me why? Two nice people who never did anybody any harm. Of course, Cookie was a pansy, but so what? If that's the way he was built I guess he couldn't help it. I'll never find another piano player like him, I'll tell you that much."

"Would you like to see the guy that did this get his lumps?"

"What do you think?" said Big Sam. "I'd like to get my hands on the dirty rat for five minutes. Just five minutes, that's all I ask."

"I've got a line on him," I said, "but I need more information and you can help me."

"How? Just tell me how," said Big Sam.

"I've got to know exactly what happened last night after I walked out. I talked to Peggy this morning before—before it happened. I also talked to the tall blonde. Now I want your version. When I put all the stories together I'll be one step closer to finding out how it happened."

"Where do I begin?"

"First, tell me about the guy who was sitting at the end of the bar."

"There isn't much to tell."

"Did you know who he was?"

"No, I didn't even get a good look at his face."

"Why not?"

"He was wearing a cap pulled down low and he had his collar turned up. Not only that, but he kept his head down low."

"Damn it," I said. "I was hoping that you'd know who he was or at least something about him."

"Is he important?"

"That's the whole thing," I said, "I don't know. But I can't afford to pass up a single lead."

"I don't think he had anything to do with it, anyway," said Big Sam. "He left before Cookie was killed."

"When?" I asked. "When did he leave? Tell me exactly."

"I can't tell you exactly because I can't remember exactly."

"Okay, then, let's go over this thing step by step."

"Hey, Sam," came a voice from the other end of the bar, "How about some service down here."

"Be right there," Sam called back. "I'll only be a minute," he said to me.

While Sam was attending to business I pulled out my cigarettes. I took one from the pack and opened my match-book. There were no matches left. I had to wait for Sam to come back. When he did I asked him for a match. He patted his pockets, then went to the back bar and brought me a book of matches.

"I don't smoke," he apologized, "but I try to keep matches on hand for my customers. Now, where were we?"

"I want you to think carefully, Sam. Tell me what everybody was doing when I walked out last night."

"I don't want to change the subject, but how come you ended up in the alley out in back?"

"I'll make it short. I was trying to pick up the blonde. She didn't want to look like a cheap pick-up so she told me to meet her out in back. While I was waiting somebody clipped me from behind and the next thing I knew, Cookie was lying dead on top of me. Now you know as much as I do. I want to know as much as you do."

"Well, when you left I think Cookie was playing your pinball machine. I was just as happy he played that as the piano. He was way off form last night. I never heard him play so badly."

"Where was the blonde?"

"At the piano bar. She sat there for a while, then she got up and went to the can."

"How do you know?"

"I didn't follow her in, if that's what you mean. I can't see around the corner but that's the direction she went."

"How do you know she didn't go to the phone? That's back there, too."

"I know that she didn't for sure because just as she was going there was a phone call for Cookie. I told him to take the call in the back."

"Who called him?"

"Some guy. Probably one of his boy friends, if you know what I mean."

"You didn't recognize the voice?" I asked.

"No, I can't say that I did. But I didn't think anything about it at the time. Cookie was always getting phone calls. Seems those guys never left him alone. I kept telling him not to have his friends call him when he was working. I really had it out with him a few days ago."

"Did it do any good?"

"Yeah. That was the first call he had since I told him off."

"And you didn't recognize the voice?"

"No," he said shaking his head. "And usually I'm pretty good at it. I just thought it was one of his boy friends."

"What did the voice sound like?"

"To tell the truth, most of them sound alike, if you know what I mean. Some higher, some lower, but they have that way of talking, polite like."

"What did the voice say?"

"It said, 'May I please talk to Cookie,' that's all."

"Now where was Peggy when this happened?"

"There wasn't too much doing so I let her off a little early."

"Before or after the call?"

"I really don't remember."

"Okay," I said, "now try to remember about the guy at the bar. When did he leave?"

"I think a few minutes after you did."

"Was that before or after the call?"

Big Sam thought a minute. "I think it was af—no, no, it was before."

"Are you sure?"

"Positive. I remember now, I just picked up his empty glass when the phone rang."

"Now this may be real important," I said, "so tax your memory. Which way did he go out?"

"I—I—gosh, Tony, I want to help, you know that. But it's impossible to remember a lot of things that happened when at the time they were unimportant and there was no reason to remember. Now, I thought he went out the front door, but it's just possible he could have gone out the back."

"That all depends," I said.

"On what?" Big Sam asked.

"On when he left," I said. "Remember, when I left, I went out the front door, down to the corner, around the corner and down the side street. That took maybe two or three minutes. If he left, say five minutes after I did I would have seen him if he came out the back way."

"I get what you're driving at," said Big Sam, "but for the life of me I couldn't tell you if it was two minutes, three minutes or five minutes. I know for sure it wasn't ten minutes, but how much less I couldn't say."

I told Big Sam to fix me another drink. So far his story was checking out with the other versions although I didn't remember Peggy mentioning the phone call. But no one can remember everything and there was no way I could question her any further. Unless, of course, Coletti got his hooks into me and sent me to the chamber. But even then I had no guarantee I'd end up in the same place Peggy did.

Sam brought my drink. He went to attend his other customers and then came back. "Am I being any help?" he asked.

"I don't know about that," I said, "but you're sure trying hard enough. Now, tell me, what did Cookie do when he came back from the phone?"

"He didn't."

"What?" I almost shouted.

"When he went to answer the phone he didn't come back."

"Didn't you go back to see what happened to him?"

"I didn't think anything about it at the time. I noticed he was gone for quite a few minutes but I thought he was having a long conversation. Sometimes, when he got a call he'd talk for ten or fifteen minutes. Just like a woman. The joint was empty anyway so it didn't make any difference to me whether or not he was on the job."

"You said the joint was empty. What about the blonde?"

"Oh," Big Sam said, "She came out of the can and walked out the front door."

"When was this?"

"Right after Cookie went to the phone."

"When did you first get worried about Cookie?"

"To tell the truth," said Big Sam, "I didn't even give him a thought until I heard the shots."

"You heard the shots?"

"Yeah, two of them. They sounded like they came from out back so I ran out the back door to see what happened."

"And what did you see?"

"Nothing at first, it was dark as hell out there. Then I noticed these two bodies lying on the ground. I didn't bother to look and see who they were. I just ran back inside and called the cops. I didn't find out until later that it was you and Cookie."

I lit another cigarette. I took a deep drag and then watched the blue smoke coil up to the ceiling. "And that's all you know?"

"That's about it," said Big Sam. "I wish I could tell you more."

"There's nothing at all that's happened before or after that you can remember? I mean anything the least little bit out of the ordinary that may or may not have anything to do with the murder."

"No," said Big Sam. "I'm positive. Unless, of course—but, no, I'm positive it had nothing to do with the murder."

"What are you talking about?" I asked with renewed interest.

"Like I said, I know this had absolutely nothing to do with the murder and it's not the first time it's happened."

"What are you talking about?" I asked on the point of exasperation.

"Somebody broke into the place last night."

"How do you know?"

"Simple. The lock on the back door was forced."

"Did they get away with anything?"

"No, I'm too smart for that," he said. "Like I said, this place has been busted into a few times before. I lost a little dough the first time but since then I've wised up. I just don't leave any loose cash laying around."

"What about your liquor?"

"I keep most of my stock locked up in the back room. When they can't find any money they usually clear out in a hurry."

"Did you report it to the police?"

"What for?" asked Big Sam. "There wasn't anything missing."

"But they might be able to find fingerprints," I said.

"They sure would," said Big Sam. "They'd find the fingerprints of all my customers. And how do you think they'd like being questioned? Especially the guys whose wives don't know they come in here. That could ruin me, you know."

"Well, I'd better get going," I said. "No sense pressing my luck by hanging around here."

"I'm sorry I couldn't help you," said Big Sam, "but there's one thing I want you to know."

"And what's that?" I asked.

Big Sam stuck out his big hairy paw. "No matter what happens, you've always got a home here for one of your pinball machines."

CHAPTER NINE

D ID YOU EVER have a funny feeling that something was going to happen? It starts with a vague uneasiness that has no meaning and then it spreads until you feel it in your groin and your stomach muscles contract. It might be in the dead of winter but you'll suddenly notice that you're sweating. That's the way I felt when I slipped out of the back door of Big Sam's.

I glanced across the alley and saw my car parked where I had told Wanda to park it. I looked and listened but saw or heard nothing in the alley to indicate there was any danger. I walked across the alley to my car and tried to open the door before I remembered that I had instructed Wanda to lock it and put the keys on top of the left front tire. I bent over to get them and as I did I caught a movement out of the corner of my eye. A split second later I heard the roar of an engine. I straightened up and whirled around. A car came roaring up the alley. It wasn't twenty feet away and it was headed directly for me. If I stayed where I was I would make a perfect target. These things ran through my mind in a fraction of a second. When I acted it was on impulse only. I threw myself up over the hood of my car and slithered across to the other side. I fell to the ground, landing on my shoulder. The impact knocked the forty-five loose and it went skidding out in front of me.

I knew I had to have the gun so I scrambled after it on all fours. Just as I reached out for it a foot came down on my hand. Hard.

A voice said, "You won't be needing that anymore."

Then I heard the sound of a car backing up and stopping, a door opening and being slammed shut and footsteps running toward me.

Then I heard another voice. This one sounded vaguely familiar. "Did you get him, Eddie?"

"Yeah," said the voice belonging to Eddie, "just the way we planned."

"Good," said the familiar voice, closer now. "All right, little man, you can get up now."

Then I knew who it was—pimple face, the punk I sent to the hospital.

I started getting to my feet when Eddie said, "Keep your hands where I can see them." I kept my hands chest high out in front of me and stood up.

"Why, he's only a little runt, Pinky," said Eddie. "Christ, from the way you described him I expected to find a giant."

"Well, I didn't get a good look at him," mumbled Pinky. "Besides he hit me from behind."

Eddie was in front of me and Pinky behind me, and they both had guns. They had me trapped so I did the only thing I could do; I burst out laughing.

"What's so damn funny?" demanded Pinky.

"How did a great big grown up two-for a nickel hood like you ever get a tag like Pinky?" I said. "And where's your knickerbockers?"

Pinky came at me with his gun raised. "Why you dirty..."

"Knock it off," said Eddie harshly. "The boss said no rough stuff. He wants this guy in condition to talk."

"He can still talk with a broken nose. I owe him one and I always pay my debts."

"Later," said Eddie. "When the boss is through with him he's your baby. But until then, behave."

"All right, little man, you just got a reprieve," said Pinky, breathing in my face. "But just remember, you and me, we got a score to settle. What you did to me is nothin' to what I'm going to do to you."

He had his face right up against mine when he finished talking so I spit in it. He jumped back, wiping his face on the sleeve of his coat, then he swung at me with his gun hand. I anticipated his swing and ducked when his hand was halfway around and he couldn't check his swing. I felt the air whistling past my face. He was swinging for the fences. He cursed and came at me again.

"I said knock it off and I mean it," said Eddie. "We got to get out of here before somebody happens along and queers the whole deal. Now, come on." He bent down and picked up the forty-five. He handed it to Pinky. "Here's your rod, let's see if you can hold on to it this time."

He prodded me toward the car, opened the door and helped me in with a shove. He climbed into the back seat with me while Pinky got in front behind the wheel.

"Keep your eye on him," Pinky called back over his shoulder as he put the car in motion, "he's a cutie."

"You keep yours on the road and I'll take care of things back here," Eddie replied, not too pleasantly.

The car negotiated the corner, drove up the street and turned to the right on Columbus.

"I don't suppose it would do any good to ask where we're going," I said.

"That's right," answered Eddie. "You'll know when we get there."

"I hope this won't take too long," I said lightly, "I've got a dinner engagement at seven."

"Now ain't that just too bad," said Pinky, sarcastically, "but when I get through with you, you'll have to eat your dinner through a straw."

"I wish you'd stop talking like that," I chided him gently, "you're liable to scare me to death."

Pinky abruptly wheeled the car into the curb and was halfway into the back seat before Eddie could stop him. His face was purple.

"Goddammit, Pinky, I'm gonna warn you just once more," said Eddie vehemently. "Knock it off and tend to your driving. Can't you see he's just baiting you? When you get mad you get careless and that's just what he wants. Now let's get going."

Pinky muttered under his breath and started the car moving again. "Just wait," he said. "Just wait, just you wait."

"I think your needle's stuck," I said.

"Awright," said Eddie, "you knock it off, too."

"Why, Eddie," I said, my voice full of mock surprise, "you sound like you're losing your temper. Naughty, naughty."

He started to say something and then clamped his mouth shut. He was determined not to let me bait him, too.

"Did Charlie mention what he wanted me for?" I asked innocently.

At the mention of Charlie's name, Pinky's head started coming around but he caught himself and concentrated on driving. Eddie remained silent.

"Do you mind if I smoke?" I said.

Eddie was noncommittal. "Suit yourself."

"I just didn't want you to get the wrong idea when I reached in my pocket," I said. "After all, I could have another rod." I reached into my pocket and fumbled around for my cigarettes. Eddie watched me very carefully. I found the pack and pulled it out quickly. Eddie jerked his gun around.

I held out the pack. "Care for one?" He started to reach for a cigarette then stopped, as though suspecting a trap. "What's the matter?" I said casually. "Wrong brand?"

"Don't care for any," he muttered.

I lit my cigarette, took a healthy drag and exhaled in an obvious display of pleasure. "That sure tastes good," I said. "Sure you won't change your mind and join me?"

"Look, wise guy," he said finally, unable to contain himself any longer, "you can wise off all you want now, but you won't think it's so funny in a little while."

"Oh, I don't know," I said, "I've got an incredible sense of humor."

"Is that right?" said Eddie. "Well, laugh this off." He raised his gun and brought it down on the side of my head. I was dizzy for a few minutes and when the initial shock wore off there was an incessant throbbing in my left temple. I touched the spot with my hand. He had raised a welt but hadn't drawn any blood.

"I've got to hand it to you Eddie," I said, "you've sure got a lot of guts. After all, all you've got to defend yourself with is a stinking little gun. You're displaying heroism above and beyond the call of duty."

"What did I tell you," sang out Pinky, "he's a regular smartass."

"We'll see how smart he acts when we finish with him," said Eddie grimly.

"Why don't we work him over right now?" said Pinky.

"You know damn well why," answered Eddie, "so shut up and drive."

"Stop giving me orders," said Pinky petulantly.

"I'll tell you what to do and you'll do it. You messed up once today, you're not going to get a second chance."

Pinky said, "I suppose you could have done better. What about the time you lost that whole shipment of—"

Eddie cut him off. "Shut your face."

We rode in silence for a while. The air in the car was charged with hostility. I figured that if I could keep the two hoods at odds with each other they might concentrate less on me. I didn't know how much good it would do but my choice of action was strictly limited. I had, actually, two choices; I could sit in the car and ride to our destination or I could wait for an opportunity to throw the door open and bolt out of there. Neither choice offered much hope. I knew what was in store for me when we finally arrived at where we were going. And if I did manage to get out of the car, then what? The answer was simple—they would come right after me. The only solace I had was the fact that obviously they were instructed to deliver me intact and in good working order.

I hadn't been paying too much attention to the route we were taking. I knew that we were still north of Market Street and that we were travelling south. Then Pinky turned right on Pine Street which was a one way street going west. Abruptly he slowed the car.

Eddie leaned forward. "What's the matter?"

"There's a cop standing on the next corner," he said.

"So keep your eye on the wise guy, so he doesn't pull a fast one."

"Are you kidding?" Eddie said derisively. "With two murder raps hanging over his head? I can just see him turning himself in."

"Well, watch him just the same."

I lit another cigarette and took stock of the situation. The cop was on the corner of the next street which was a one way street heading south. We were travelling in the curb lane slowly as Pinky was trying to maneuver the car into the middle lane to put some distance between us and the cop. He couldn't do it because there were cars behind us and to our left. As we approached the corner the signal light changed from green to yellow. The car in front of us made it across on the change. Pinky couldn't afford to take any unnecessary risks. He brought the car to a stop.

I watched the signal light that controlled the flow of traffic on the street that intersected the one we were on. I waited until it flashed yellow and then I made my move.

I flipped my lighted cigarette into Eddie's face. Instinctively he threw his hands up to protect himself. I opened the door, stepped out, and slammed it shut. I waved to the two hoods and said, loud enough for the cop to hear. "Thanks for the ride, fellas, I sure appreciate it."

They sat there glowering unable to decide what to do. The cars in back of them made the decision for them. The light had turned green and horns started blaring urging them to move on.

I stepped up onto the sidewalk and said, "Evening officer, nice night isn't it."

He replied, "Sure is."

I smiled and took off down the street. Pinky had no choice but to continue up Pine. He couldn't turn right and take off after me because it was a one way street. There was a possibility that he might circle the block and come looking for me.

I didn't intend to be found. I hurried down to the next corner, crossed the street and went into a drug store. I went to the phone booth in the rear of the store and called for a cab. While I waited for it, I kept to the back of the store so as to be out of sight. From where I was standing I could watch the traffic moving by outside but it would be difficult for anyone in a car to spot me because they would be past the place where I was standing before I could be visible and then they would have to know just where to look.

In a few minutes I saw a green sedan drive by slowly. I ducked back out of the way. When I looked again, it was gone.

The cab pulled up shortly. I walked out of the drug store and got into the cab. "Paoli's, please," I said as I sat back.

"Paoli's?" said the driver. "Hell, you coulda walked it. It's only a couple of blocks."

CHAPTER TEN

AOLI'S, AT SEVEN O'CLOCK on any given night, is a symphony of organized confusion. At that time of the evening space at the bar is at a premium and the eager customers are lined up three deep. To add to the confusion, the narrow space between the bar and the opposite partition serves as the only passageway from the dining room to the rest rooms. Throw in a few busboys passing out hot hors d'oeuvres and you haven't got the kind of place where people are apt to be looking for suspected murderers. Besides, the food is always excellent.

I fought my way to the bar and ordered a drink. I looked for Lorna but I didn't expect to find her because, despite the unpleasant interruption, I was early. I finished my drink and collared the busy head waiter. I told him I was expecting a young lady and asked him to reserve the most secluded table on the mezzanine. I told him I wanted it available on a moment's notice.

He told me he would do the best he could under the circumstances so I slipped him the folded ten spot I had ready. He permitted his granite features to break into a slight smile and assured me that my gesture was entirely unnecessary as he discreetly made the bill vanish.

Lorna arrived promptly at seven. Even in that madhouse I had no trouble finding her. She was the kind of a woman that would stand out in any crowd. We didn't say much until we were seated at our table and it was Lorna who fired the first salvo.

She said, "Do you think it's wise for you to come to a place like this?"

"You should have thought of that this afternoon," I said.

She blushed, very prettily. "I—I guess I wasn't thinking too clearly. I'm sorry. Would you like to go somewhere else?"

"Hell, no," I answered her. "Who would think of looking for me in a place like this?"

"I never looked at it that way," she said, "but you're still taking an awful risk being out in public."

"And what about you?" I asked. "If I get caught while you're with me, how does that make you look?"

"If I was worried about that I wouldn't be here now."

"I'm glad you said that."

The waiter approached our table so we halted our conversation while I ordered. After he left, I said, "You know I don't like to beat around the bush ... "

Her features took on a concerned look. "What is it, Tony?"

"Your story of what took place at Big Sam's last night checks out." She sighed in relief. "But," I continued, "there's one thing that still bothers me."

"Tell me what it is, Tony. You know I have no secrets from you." She looked directly at me as she spoke and I felt a tingle in my spine as I recalled the proof she had offered me earlier in the day.

"What do you know about Charlie Yee?"

She frowned. "Nothing, I'm afraid. Should I know something?"

"That depends ... "

She laughed. "I know—on whether or not I'm telling the truth."

"You're certain you've never heard of Charlie Yee? You've never heard the name mentioned before in any way, shape or form?"

"You sound like a prosecuting attorney."

"Maybe so," I said, "but I've also got to act as judge and jury. And after all the evidence is in, I have to make a decision."

"What kind of a decision?"

"Whether or not to trust you," I said, "completely."

"I hope the decision is favorable," she said. "I do so want you to trust me. Despite the evidence to the contrary, I have complete faith in the fact that you're not mixed up in any murders. If I was to believe what people say and what is printed in the newspapers, I wouldn't be able to believe in you. But I do and you know I do. I wish you would have the same blind confidence in me."

"I want to. Believe me, I want to. I haven't felt toward a woman the way I feel toward you for a long, long time. But I got hurt pretty badly when I lost her. I wouldn't want it to happen again. That's why I've got to be so sure of you."

She said, "Tell me about this Charlie Yee business and why you think I should know about him."

"When I spoke to Peggy this morning she told me you had been in Big Sam's on a number of occasions."

"That's right," she said, "I told you that myself. I went there because I enjoyed Cookie's music."

"I asked her if she ever heard any conversation between you two and she remembered overhearing only one phrase, 'Charlie eel make a deal.' "

" 'Charlie eel make a deal?' " she repeated. "It doesn't make any sense."

"It didn't to me either until I was able to connect it up later."

"How?" she asked.

"Before I tell you that, or anything else for that matter, I've got to be completely convinced that you know nothing about it."

"I don't know how I can convince you," she said. "Who was supposed to have said it, me or Cookie?"

"I don't know," I said, "I didn't think to ask Peggy at the time and now it's too late."

"Do you think it's possible that Peggy heard the conversation Cookie had with someone else and somehow connected it with me?"

"Anything's possible," I said, "although I've always found Peggy very reliable."

She shook her head in bewilderment. "I've told you that I know nothing about Charlie Yee or Charlie eel. Other than that I can tell you nothing. Now it's up to you. You can choose either to believe me or not to believe me."

She spoke so earnestly, with such an air of sincerity that I wondered why I ever doubted her. I decided then and there to take her into my confidence.

The waiter brought food and a bottle of wine. Lorna took my hand in hers and held it tightly while the waiter arranged the various dishes on the table. Despite the fact that I was wanted by the police and hunted by some hoods, I had a feeling that everything was right with the world. If a feeling of doubt started to assert itself I had only to look at Lorna's wistful smile to become reassured.

We were sitting in one of the few booths on the mezzanine and while the waiter had been busy with the table, Lorna had edged around the upholstered seat until she was right next to me. She rubbed her thigh against mine while she was moving and at that magical moment my thoughts were far removed from murders, hoods and loot. I felt like an ordinary guy with an extraordinary date. I looked around at the other tables to see if I could find another woman whose attributes could compare with Lorna's. There was none. I felt warm and expansive, a feeling bolstered by the good table wine.

After we started eating, Lorna asked, "Are you making any headway in finding the real murderer?"

"Some," I said, "but it's slow going."

"My goodness," she said, "it's been less than twenty-four hours. How much can you accomplish in one day?"

"That isn't the point," I said. "It's how long can I elude the police and Charlie Yee's gang."

"There's that name again," she said, smiling. "Do you want to tell me about it now?"

"Yes," I said, "I've got to talk it over with someone to get the facts straight in my own mind. This whole thing started a couple of years ago and it's tied in with that famous armored car robbery. Do you remember it?"

"Oh, yes, very well. I followed that case very closely."

"Is that right? How much of it do you remember?"

"Everything," she said. "As a matter of fact, I thought about it today."

I raised my eyebrows. "How come?"

"Because I saw the parallel between what happened in that case and what's happening to you."

"How do you mean?" I asked.

"If you'll remember," she began, speaking rapidly and with an ease showing she had discussed this many times before, "there was a question of circumstantial evidence and mistaken identity."

"You're beginning to sound like S. H. Bertram."

"I can't help that, it's just that I happened to agree with his defense of Mr. Lawrence."

"You mean Angel Face."

"Call him what you will," she said, "but there never was any positive identification of him. The witnesses merely testified that Mr. Lawrence looked like one of the gang and was dressed about the same. But not one of them could make a real positive identification."

"They were pretty sure until Bertram started his cross-examination."

"Exactly," she said triumphantly, "and then they backtracked. He got them to admit that they didn't get a look at his face and therefore it would be impossible to make a positive identification."

"They did make a positive identification of the other two, though," I said, "and he was part of the gang, assumed to be the leader."

"That's right," she countered, "but it was an erroneous assumption. If you'll recall, neither one of the other two gang members identified Mr. Lawrence as being with them or even knowing him for that matter."

"Certainly," I said, "why should they? They didn't even admit that they were there or had anything to do with the hold-up."

"But even after they were convicted and sent to San Quentin, they didn't change their story. Now, don't you think," she said, "that if Mr. Lawrence was guilty, it would just be human nature for the other two to resent being locked up while he was out free?"

"He wasn't exactly absolved," I reminded her, "he merely made good a daring escape."

"Well, it's the same thing," she said impatiently. "The fact is, until this day they haven't linked Mr. Lawrence with the crime."

"Of course not," I said, "and let me explain why. Those two boys are sitting in death row awaiting execution. Meanwhile, there's a long involved legal battle going on trying to reverse the verdict. If they admit anything now, they're just assuring themselves of a quick trip to the gas chamber."

"I hadn't looked at it that way," said Lorna, pensively, "but what about this: supposing they were to admit that Mr. Lawrence was the leader of the gang and that he was the one who killed the guard, wouldn't it go easier on them?"

"Not necessarily," I said, "they're still accessories and as such, subject to the same penalties."

Lorna took a bite of her food and contemplated silently.

I said, "I guess you did follow the case rather closely. It's odd that you should remember the facts so clearly after two years."

"It's not odd at all," she said defensively, "it's just that it made a lasting impression on me. I feel very strongly about injustice. Look at your position now. If I was to believe in circumstantial evidence, I couldn't reconcile myself to your innocence. It's the same sort of situation."

"Hardly," I said, "but I won't argue that point now."

"I'm sorry," she said, "I really shouldn't get so wound up. But what has that case got to do with this one?"

"Your memory of that other case is so good; tell me, how was that guard killed?"

"Why," she began, "why, his neck was broken."

"Exactly," I said, "you're batting a thousand per cent. Now tell me how Cookie and Peggy were killed."

"They had their necks broken, too," she said, then added hastily, "but you don't mean to say..."

I cut her off. "Why not? It's what the police call modus operandi. The crimes were committed the same way, hence the same criminal."

"Oh, but surely, you don't believe that, do you? What you're saying is that every time someone gets shot here in San Francisco, only one man would be responsible."

"Not in the least," I said. "That would depend entirely upon the circumstances surrounding the shooting. And besides, you haven't heard it all."

"There's more?"

"Lots more," I said. "I have reason to believe that the deaths of Cookie and Peggy were connected with the missing half a million dollars in the robbery."

The blood drained from her face and her eyes grew wide. I was sorry that I had to disillusion her. I knew how it felt to believe in something strongly only to have it all blown away like a wisp of smoke.

"Are you sure?" she said, finally.

"Not positive, no," I said, "but I have every reason to believe that's the case. And if my theory is correct, I'll have the proof of it tonight."

"What kind of proof?"

"A half of million dollars worth of proof."

"But, how?"

I pulled the key out of my pocket and dropped it on the table. She looked at it curiously and then picked it up and examined it more closely. She turned it around in her hand, put it back on the table and turned to me with a puzzled expression on her beautiful face.

"What does it open?" she asked.

"Shorty seems to think it's a key to a locker such as you find in bus terminals and train depots."

"Shorty?"

"He's that tall, lanky string bean that was in Big Sam's with me last night. You remember, he stopped by where I was sitting and told me he was all through? He wanted me to leave when I was trying to make out with you?"

"Oh, yes," she said, "I remember, now." Then she grew wistful. "Maybe you should have gone with him, then you wouldn't be in all this trouble now."

"Maybe," I said, "but then it might have taken me longer to get acquainted with you."

She smiled a sad little smile. "Am I worth all this?"

"All this and more."

"This Shorty, he works for you?"

"My right hand man. I couldn't get along without him. I have this pinball route and Shorty keeps all the machines in working order. That's where this key came from, the machine I have in Big Sam's."

"How did it get there?"

"Cookie was fooling around the machine last night. I believe he dropped the key in the coin slot. He was afraid of something last night. He told me his life was in danger but I didn't believe him. Maybe he thought that whoever was going to kill him was going to kill him for the key and as long as he didn't have it on him, he would be safe for a little while."

"If you think that key will unlock the mystery of the missing money, how do you account for Cookie having it in his possession?"

"Here is where I have to theorize," I said, "with a little help from the police department. The bank had the serial numbers of all the currency in that armored truck. Lately a few of the bills have turned up, all in North Beach. The police seem to think that Cookie was used to pass those bills."

"And what do you think?"

"I don't know," I said, "I just don't know. Somehow, I can't conceive of Cookie being mixed up in all this. Yet the evidence seems to point to the contrary even if it is inconsistent with his character."

"What evidence?" Loran asked.

"I found out the Cookie was making inquiries about a trip to South America. So the way it looks now is that Cookie was being used to pass the bills but he got greedy and wanted it all for himself. So he stashed the money away in a safe place until he could complete his arrangements to leave the country."

"But how would he get the money out of the country? Wouldn't his baggage be subject to customs inspection?"

"Yes," I said, "and that's probably why he didn't leave before he got knocked off."

"But where did he get the money?" asked Lorna.

"That should be fairly apparent," I said. "The only man who could have given him the money is the man who stole it in the first place, Angel Face Lawrence."

"But you're assuming that Lawrence is the guilty one. What if he was just the victim of circumstances, like you are now?"

"In either case I've got to find a phantom. If it turns out not to be Lawrence, you won't have to be disillusioned, and he'll be cleared automatically. But if it is Lawrence and I find him ... "

"What's going to happen?"

"One of us has to die," I said somberly.

Lorna shuddered. "Do you have to be so grim?"

"You're a great believer in justice," I said, "I'm just going to see to it that he doesn't have a chance to cheat justice again."

We finished our meal in silence. Somehow, the enchantment I had felt earlier had disappeared, but something else had moved in to take its place; the feeling that two people can communicate closely with each other without saying a word. Lorna would glance up at me occasionally with tenderness and compassion overflowing her eyes. Once, she leaned toward me and kissed me gently on the cheek, oblivious of the people around us.

The waiter cleared our table and brought us coffee. I offered Lorna a cigarette and took one myself. I lit hers and then started to light my own with the same match but it went out. I reached for another match but when I did I noticed something written on the inside of the match book. It was the name, Harley Perkins, and an address written in pencil. It was the match book that Big Sam had given me so I assumed that one of his customers had left it on the bar and Big Sam had, very frugally, saved it. I would have thought nothing of it until I closed the cover to strike the match.

It had advertising on it and I very seldom pay any attention to match book advertising. I did to that one. It said, "Charlie Yee, Fine Art Objects."

Lorna noticed my preoccupation with the match book and she leaned over to get a closer look. "There's that name again," she said.

"Dammed if it isn't. It keeps cropping up all over the place. I wouldn't be surprised to find it on the label of my underwear."

"You still haven't told me how he fits into the picture."

I said, "I wish I knew. This morning I had a visit from a pimply-faced hood. He used the same corny 'special delivery' routine on me that I used on you. Only difference was he got the special delivery—to a hospital. I wanted the cops to shake him down but by the time the hospital had him patched up he had an attorney there. Claimed he was paying a business call on me and I beat him up without any provocation."

Lorna was indignant. "The nerve of him."

"That wasn't all, he signed an assault and battery charge against me."

"How could he?" Lorna asked, incredulous.

"You can do anything if you've got a smart attorney, and he had a smart one."

"Who was it?" she asked.

"S. H. Bertram."

Lorna looked at me wide-eyed. I said, "Do you want to hear the rest of it?" She nodded her head.

"I called on Bertram this afternoon."

"Weren't you afraid he would call the police?"

"I gambled on that and won. He might have called the police until I dropped a little bombshell in his lap."

"What kind of a bombshell?" Lorna asked.

"I told him I knew where the missing half a million bucks was and I walked out on him. Before I did, though, I let it slip that I was parked in the Union Square Garage. As soon as I left his office I tricked his receptionist into leaving the outer office and I listened to a very interesting conversation on the extension phone."

I told Lorna about the conversation I overheard and about my subsequent visit to Charlie Yee. "So you see," I said, when I completed the story, "there's a very definite tie-in between Bertram and Charlie Yee and the half a million. And we know of the relationship between Bertram and Angel Face Lawrence, so how innocent does you martyred friend look now?"

Lorna didn't say anything. She started to speak a few times, then changed her mind.

The waiter set a little tray down in front of me, containing the check. I counted out enough money for the check and a tip.

"Would you like a little after dinner drink?" I asked Lorna.

"No," she said absently, still lost in thought. Then, "Tony..."

"Yes?"

"Would you hate me if you found out I'd lied to you?"'

I took her hand and looked into her eyes. "I couldn't hate you if I wanted to. I'll admit that my thoughts weren't too charitable this morning when I thought you had something to do with making a patsy of me. In fact, I was ready to work you over, woman or no woman."

"I had nothing to do with what happened last night," she said, "you must believe that."

"I do believe it," I said. "You don't have to repeat it."

"But I want you to be sure of it, regardless of what happens." She was trembling as she spoke.

"Honey," I said. "Baby, take it easy, I told you I believe you. I also believe you couldn't do anything to harm anyone if you tried. Now, take it easy." I put my arm around her and she nestled her head on my shoulder.

I waited until her trembling subsided and then I cupped her chin in my hand and tilted her head back. I brushed her cheek with my lips.

"Do you want to tell me what this is all about?" I said, gently.

"Oh, Tony, I'm afraid I've fallen in love with you. Silly, isn't it?"

"What's silly about it? I think it's kind of nice."

"But we hardly know each other."

"I know as much about you as I need to know."

"No," she said, "you don't. You don't know nearly enough."

"Suppose you let me be the judge of that. Now, what's this deep dark secret you're keeping from me? Do you have a husband in Peoria? Did you resent your mother and hate your father?"

"Please, Tony," she implored, "don't make a joke of it."

"A little while ago you accused me of being grim; now who's being grim?"

"I'm sorry," she said and then she forced a little laugh. "It seems as though I'm spending half the evening apologizing to you."

"Yes," I said, "and it's all very unnecessary. Look, sweetheart, if you don't want to talk about whatever it is that's weighing on your conscience, you don't have to."

"I do want to—but I can't. Not yet, anyway. Oh, God," she said, rubbing her temples, "why must things be so complicated?"

"Things really aren't complicated, it's only that people make them so. You'll see, when all this is over, that there was a natural sequence of events leading to the murders. The answers will be so simple I'll wonder why they didn't jump up and hit me in the face. The facts are all here, it's just that I haven't been able to interpret them yet.

"It's like trying to draw the picture of a man whose features are partly concealed. You can guess at the hidden features and even have someone describe them to you, but the picture just won't come out right. Maybe the nose is too long or the ears too short—do you follow what I mean?"

She nodded. "I wish I could help you draw that picture." She mused for a moment. "Perhaps I can," she said softly. "You've got the outline, maybe I can fill in the highlights for you."

I put my hands on her shoulders and turned her so that she was facing me directly. "Lorna, you've been trying to tell me something and you've been talking all around it. I can't force you to tell me and I wouldn't force you if I could. But I wish you would tell me—you'd feel a lot better for it."

She turned away from me and wiped a tear from the corner of her eye. Then she turned back with a brave smile. "Tony," she whispered huskily, "where are you going when you leave here?"

"I'm going to try to find that money and see if it brings me any closer to the solution of this thing."

"Do you have to do that tonight?"

"The sooner the better—I'm fighting against time. Why do you ask?"

"Because I'm afraid that having just found you I'm in danger of losing you."

"Don't you worry about this baby," I said. "I may be smaller than standard but that just makes me a smaller target."

"Don't go," she said, "stay with me—stay with me for the rest of the night—I'm frightened."

"I wish I could so don't tempt me. It would almost be worth the gas chamber."

"You're laughing at me again."

"I was never more serious in my life," I said. "Do you think I enjoy getting belted on the head, having a gun stuck in my ribs? Do you think it's any fun setting myself up like a duck in a shooting gallery hoping that the guy who pulls the trigger has a bad eye?

"Look at me—I don't want you to miss a word. When this is all over—and I hope to God it's soon—I'm going to take you down to Carmel. There's a little place I know of, where you can hear the ocean come roaring in like a thousand freight trains and then when it's spent itself on the beach you can hear it tiptoeing away like a satisfied lover. You can look straight ahead for a hundred years and see nothing but water and sky and you can use that hundred years to taste just one kiss."

"Take me there tonight, now," said Lorna softly. "No one would ever guess we were there. Let the police fight their own battles."

"That's one of the problems," I said, "the police seem to think that I'm one of their battles."

"Tony, will you promise me one thing?"

"Anything. You name it."

"Promise me that no matter what happens you'll believe in me and believe that I love you."

I said, "That's a simple request but I don't understand why … "

"I can't explain, not now. Will you promise me?"

"Of course, but ... "

Lorna interrupted me again. "Don't ask me anything. I don't want to lie to you. You made me a promise, now I'll make you one. I have to find something out first, but as soon as I do I'll tell you all about it."

"When?"

"I should know tonight."

I said, "That's good enough for me. Now, before I get too used to this easy living, we'd better go. Shall I take you home?"

"No, I have a car. It isn't much, but it gets me where I want to go."

We got up from the table and made our way back downstairs. I saw Lorna to the California Street entrance and then I went to the phone. I called the cab company and requested cab number seven eleven. The dispatcher gave me a little jazz but finally agreed to send Joe Pinsky over as soon as he could locate him via the two-way radio. He told me it wouldn't be over fifteen minutes.

I went to the bar and ordered a King Alphonse in the rough. While I sipped the drink I tried to figure out what Lorna was trying to tell me. I was beginning to regret not insisting that she tell me. I wondered if she knew something I should know but I was certain she would tell me if she did. Possibly, I thought, it was a personal problem. She was a strange one, all right, but that was part of her charm; the mystery about her that made her so appealing. I promised myself that that was one mystery I would solve—and soon.

I finished my drink and checked the time. Close to fifteen minutes had passed so I decided to check outside to see if Joe had arrived. Actually, any cab would have gotten the job done, but I had a few stops to make and there was no sense risking recognition by another alert cabbie.

I stepped out into the brisk night air and filled my lungs with it. Before I had a chance to exhale I felt something pressing against my back and I heard a voice saying, "I hope you enjoyed your dinner because in about fifteen minutes you're going to be puking it up."

CHAPTER ELEVEN

I DIDN'T HAVE to turn around to find out who was poking a gun in my back. I said, "Pinky, you're beginning to annoy me. I wish you would stop following me around."

I moved my foot backwards, slowly, until I could feel the toe of his shoe. Then quickly I raised my foot and brought it down as hard as I could on top of his. He let out a yelp as I whirled around with a clenched fist. I caught him flush on the jaw. I didn't wait to see if I knocked him out. I sprinted for the corner.

I might have expected what happened next. As I wheeled around the corner a foot shot out in front of me but I saw it too late to stop. I tripped and fell headlong onto the sidewalk. Before I had a chance to get to my feet, Eddie raised his gun and brought it down viciously on the back of my head.

They strapped me down in the chair and the warden said solemnly, "Anthony Ceaser, do you have anything to say before execution is carried out?" Then he laughed uproariously and he sounded exactly like Charlie Yee. He started to puff up like a balloon and soon he even looked like Charlie Yee. "My that's a silly name," he intoned, "Anthony Ceaser." And he repeated it until the name sounded as if it were coming from an echo chamber. "Well, Anthony Ceaser, have you nothing to say, nothing to say, nothing to say … " I tried to talk but there was a big wad of cotton stuffed in my mouth. The warden stepped back and said, "Carry out the execution." I waited to hear the splash of the pellets in the acid and the hiss of escaping gas but instead the walls started closing in on me until I was wedged in so tightly I couldn't move. Then the upper part of the walls broke off and crashed against my head where they pressed relentlessly until my head throbbed violently. Then suddenly a trap door sprung open and I felt myself falling. I fell endlessly into a black bottomless void. I felt something rough and coarse around my throat. I touched it with my hands and found out it was a rope. In a panic I waited for the rope to run out and jerk my head back until my neck was broken. I felt the slack taken up on the rope and waited in terror for the inevitable. I tried to rip the rope from around my neck but by now my hands were paralyzed and I couldn't move them. The rope finally ran out and my head jerked back—but the rope snapped and I fell free, right into the middle of the Pacific Ocean. A voice said, "He's coming around. I told you that bucket of water would do the trick."

Consciousness flooded in on a sea of nausea. I was lying sprawled out on the floor of a storeroom. There were packing cases arranged around the walls and a work bench in the middle of the room over which dangled a naked electric light. There was a carton of shiny tin cans on the table and a small home-type canning machine.

There were also three pairs of shoes on the floor and they were filled with feet.

The owner of one pair of shoes said, "Did you search him thoroughly?" The voice and the shoes belonged to Charlie Yee.

"Yeah," said Eddie, "but we couldn't find it."

"Bring him to his feet," said Charlie, "we shall have a little discussion."

Eddie and Pinky each helped themselves to an arm and jerked me to an upright position.

"Good evening, Mr. Ceaser," said Charlie, cordially. "It is regrettable that we must meet again under such unfortunate circumstances. I hope we haven't inconvenienced you too much."

I didn't answer him, not because I didn't want to but because my tongue felt like a pregnant snake wearing a woolen overcoat.

And my head wasn't in the best possible shape. It pained me even when I frowned—and I was in no mood to smile.

"Now, then," continued Charlie, "if you will turn over to us a useless little key there will be no further reason to detain you."

I tried to talk but it was useless. I think I managed to convey the idea that a glass of water would help. Charlie brought me one, which I downed gratefully.

"Can you speak now?" asked Charlie. I nodded my head. "Good," he said, "now suppose you tell us where we can obtain a certain key."

"Try a locksmith," I cracked.

"My patience is wearing thin and I can no longer find you amusing," Charlie said, coldly.

"So don't laugh," I said.

Charlie nodded to his two goons. Eddie stepped around behind me and pinioned my arms. Pinky took his coat off.

Pinky said, "I was hoping you'd be stubborn." He cocked his arm and gave me a right hook to the ribs. The next one was to the pit of my stomach. The nausea, which had begun to vanish, rushed back. I fought a desperate urge to vomit. Pinky moved in and prepared to paste me again. I waited until he was right in front of me and I let go. I threw my head forward and aimed for his face.

He was a mess. Paoli's excellent cuisine didn't look good on him at all. He brought his gun out and would have shot me on the spot if it wasn't for a terse command from Charlie.

"Enough!" he hissed. "Now go clean yourself. You look and smell like a swine."

Pinky left the room muttering darkly.

"You will be able to save yourself an enormous amount of discomfort," Charlie said, "if you choose not to be stubborn. For your own good I would suggest you assume a reasonable attitude."

"Then what happens?" I asked.

"If you choose to cooperate, it will be needless for you to suffer any further discomfort and as soon as we have the key you will be free to go."

I said, "Now who's being a comedian? I can just picture you letting me go."

Charlie said, "Why not? You can't very well go to the police so it would be useless for us to complicate matters by disposing of you."

"It might be useless to dispose of me if it complicated matters, but what if it didn't complicate matters. What if it just made things delightfully simple for you?"

"How so?"

"By bumping me off and making it look like suicide. 'The murderer was remorseful over his crimes.' But I'm certain that thought couldn't possibly have occurred to you."

Charlie's eyes narrowed. "You leave me no alternative but to resort to violence. I find it most distasteful. All right, Eddie."

Eddie let go of my left arm and concentrated on the right. He twisted it behind my back exerting an upward pressure. A cold sweat broke out on my forehead. He pushed it higher and higher while I tried to writhe out of his grip but the more I struggled the more intense the pain became. I clamped my teeth on my lower lip until I tasted blood. The pain was excruciating.

Charlie was watching my face intently for a sign that I was cracking but the only sign of cracking came from my arm. Only it sounded more like a "pop."

"Jeez," swore Eddie. "I broke his arm … "

If he said anything else I didn't hear it. I passed out.

Consciousness returned slowly this time and with it, intense pain. I was lying on the floor again and had the same view of the packing cases and the table. Only this time, no shoes, for which I was grateful. I pulled myself to a sitting position and rested for a few minutes. Eddie had been wrong on his diagnosis of my arm. It wasn't broken—the shoulder was dislocated and it hurt like hell.

I pulled myself to my feet and started looking for a way to get out of there. There was a small door in the corner to my right, through which, I surmised, my antagonists had gone. I looked around the rest of the room and found a huge sliding door at one end. It was locked but at least I was able to determine that there was a street of some kind on the other side of the door. To the right of the door, about six feet up was a window.

I pushed a packing case up against the wall beneath the window and another smaller case against the first one to make a step. I was about to climb up when I heard footsteps and voices. I hurried back to where I had been lying on the floor and tried to assume the same position. There was a steady intense throbbing in my shoulder and my right arm was completely useless.

I heard the door open and the footsteps coming over to where I was prostrated on the floor.

"He's still out," said Eddie.

"Why in the hell did you do that for?" Pinky asked, annoyed. "I wanted to work him over myself."

"Maybe you are forgetting our purpose," came Charlie's voice. "Without that key our entire project is at a standstill. Are you sure you searched him thoroughly?"

"I'll say we did," said Pinky, "while he was out the first time. He was carrying quite a roll. At least Eddie and I don't have to work for nothing."

"Chicken feed," said Charlie disdainfully. "He holds the key to a fortune and you satisfy yourselves with a paltry few dollars."

"What did you want us to do, leave it on him?" asked Eddie. "Where he's going he won't need any money."

"He is going nowhere until we have that key. I simply do not have the stomach for brutality. I shall be in my office when you need me."

"But what do you expect us to do?" asked Eddie. "He may be a runt, but he's tough—I've gotta hand it to him."

"Every man has a breaking point," said Charlie. "The human body can absorb only so much punishment before the mind informs it it has had enough. He is no different than anyone else. It is just a matter of torture and time. Now get busy—I want results and I don't care how you obtain them."

"Leave it to me," said Pinky. "I'll make him wish he was dead. Before I get through with him he'll be begging me to kill him and put him out of his misery. I've had all I can take from that smart little bastard and now he's gonna get his."

Charlie said, "At least you are in the proper frame of mind. Now get busy." I heard his footsteps retreating and the opening and closing of a door.

The outlook wasn't very pleasant. The only consolation I had was that as long as they didn't have the key they wouldn't kill me. It was small consolation in view of the punishment I had received and could count on receiving.

Then I had a disquieting thought. Why hadn't they found the key? It should have been in my pocket. Maybe it had dropped out when I was tripped in front of Paoli's. I dismissed that as unlikely. The last I remembered of the key was when I showed it to Lorna. Had she kept it? I didn't recall her handing it back to me. She had picked it up and examined it and then what did she do? Of course, she put it back on the table and I hadn't picked it up. Then it became obvious what must have happened. When the waiter brought the check he must have set the little tray down on top of the key and hidden it from view. That little gesture had probably saved my life—or at least, prolonged it. If they had found the key on me—

"Let's try some more water," suggested Eddie.

"Naw," said Pinky, "he's probably faking. Which arm did you say you broke?"

"His right."

"Okay," said Pinky, "we'll see if he's faking." He bent down, grabbed my arm and gave it a twist. I tried to contain myself but I couldn't help crying out.

"What did I tell ya?" asked Pinky proudly. "Pick him up."

Eddie grabbed me under the armpits and hoisted me to my feet. I winced with pain as he exerted pressure on my right shoulder.

"Now, that's better," said Pinky with a big toothy grin. "You just hold him upright and we're gonna have us some fun." He turned serious for a moment. "I hope you're gonna be stubborn. I hope you just don't say one word about that stinkin' key—not for a long while."

He spit into each of his palms like a baseball player about to take his turn at bat. Then he cut loose and hit me on the fleshy part of my nose. Blood spurted out and covered the front of my shirt. I grew dizzy and weak but Eddie wouldn't let me slump to the floor—he held me upright.

"That's one I owe you," Pinky said, "and here's another one." This time he hit me in the eye. He followed that up with a kidney punch and another blow to my face. Fortunately, I passed out again.

There was more—I don't know much more. Pinky worked me over gleefully while I was conscious, semi-conscious and probably when I was out. I don't remember how many times I was out nor what took place in between times. I believe Charlie returned once to check on the progress. He said something that didn't make much sense, or perhaps I was delirious and only imagined it.

But it seemed to me I heard him say, "He's holding up the shipment of shrimp."

There was a long period when I remembered absolutely nothing. I must have been out, but good—or maybe Pinky was getting arm weary. I was about ready to give up. I was in a state where I didn't care if they killed me or not, it wouldn't have made much difference.

I don't remember regaining consciousness the last time but a plan was beginning to formulate itself in the dark recesses of my mind. It kept pushing itself forward and fading out again.

I began groaning. There was immediate activity. Eddie hauled me to my feet again.

"Are you ready to talk, wise guy, or do you want more?" asked Pinky.

"Give me a drink of water," I mumbled.

"Sure thing," said Pinky agreeably. He got a glass of water and held it a few inches in front of my lips. I leaned forward to get it and he abruptly pulled it away. "Wait a minute," he said, "maybe it's contaminated or something. I'd better check it."

He drank most of it down, then wiped his mouth with the back of his hand. "Naw, it's all right, have some." He threw the remainder of the water in my face. "Now, if you want more all you have to do is tell us where we can find that little old key. That's all, and I'll give you a nice cool drink of water. How's that, old sport."

"Okay," I whispered hoarsely, "you win."

Pinky's face wore a triumphant look. "What did I tell ya?" he asked Eddie. "He's not so tough." Then he turned back to me. "Okay, spill it."

I started talking but I purposely garbled what I was saying in a low voice.

"Speak up," demanded Pinky. "I can't hear ya."

"I can't," I whispered.

Pinky moved closer so he could hear me. I waited until he was directly in front of me and I lashed out with my foot. I kicked his shin bone. He let out a yell and then came for me with blood in his eyes. After the merciless beating he had given me he thought that he had surely knocked all the fight out of me. I had humiliated him once too often and he was ready to annihilate me—which was just what I wanted. I just hoped that the beating I had taken hadn't ruined my sense of timing. I had only one chance and I couldn't afford to muff it.

Pinky swung at me blindly, with all his strength. I waited until his fist was inches away from my face and I ducked my head fast. Eddie, who was holding me from behind, had no warning. Pinky's fist caught him on the jaw. I bent my knees, lowered my head and then straightened up when I judged my head to be under Pinky's chin. He went flying backwards.

I didn't wait to see how much damage had been inflicted on my two playmates. I ran for the window. I didn't realize how weakened the brutal beating had left me. I hoped I had enough strength to make it. I jumped onto the first packing case, stepped up to the higher one and then I plunged headlong through the window.

It was a six foot drop. I landed on my good left shoulder and rolled with the fall amid the splinters of broken glass. I had landed in a deserted alley. I glanced in both directions and headed for the nearest street. I lurched into a stumbling, lop-sided drunken run. I made the end of the alley but before I was able to draw a relieved breath, I ran into a pair of waiting outstretched arms.

CHAPTER TWELVE

COULDN'T SEE whose arms were wrapped around me but I felt myself being propelled toward a car parked at the curb. I was half pulled, half shoved into the back seat. The car gunned away from the curb. I had shut my eyes when I hit the back seat. It felt so good I wanted to keep them shut but I forced them open.

There was something familiar about the back of the driver's head. Then I saw Joe Pinsky's smiling face watching me in the mirror. I was never so happy to see anyone in my life. I told him so.

"Crimeny," he said, "what in the hell happened to you. You look like you've been put through a meat grinder."

"I'll clue you," I said, "I was."

He said, "We'll fix that right up."

"How?"

"I'm taking you to a doctor."

I shook my head. "No dice."

"Why?"

"I can't answer any questions, you know that."

"You can't walk around in that condition, either. What happened anyway?"

"I got worked over pretty good. I think my right shoulder is dislocated."

"What about your face? It's all over blood."

"I must have cut it diving through a window."

"Man, you need medical attention—bad. Don't you know a doctor who can keep his mouth shut?"

"Yeah," I said, "but he's in Las Vegas."

"I could take you to my place but my wife can't keep her damn mouth shut."

"And we can't go to my place, the cops probably have it staked out. Say," I said as a sudden thought struck me, "I know where we can go." I gave him Lorna's address.

I said, "Now that we've got that settled suppose you tell me how you came to be waiting for me at the end of that alley."

"Well," Joe began, "I got this call to pick up a fare at Paoli's. The dispatcher told me the fare insisted on my cab. Right away I figured it was you. I was way on the other side of town so I drove like mad to get there. Just as I was pulling up to the place I seen you go tearing around the corner. Then this guy trips you and slugs you with his rod. In the meantime, this other guy shows up and they dump you in this car. And, what I mean, this all happens in less than a minute. Those boys worked fast.

"Now, I coulda called the cops by calling the dispatcher on the radio but I figured that was just as bad. So I had no other choice but to follow them."

"How come they didn't spot you," I said, "and try to lose you?"

Joe tapped his head with his forefinger. "Because I got it here," he said. "I didn't tail them too close—that's always a tip-off. I always managed to stay far enough behind so they wouldn't get suspicious but not too far to take a chance on losing them. Damn near did, though, at a stop light, but lucky for me I caught them at the next one."

"You mean lucky for me," I said.

"Oh, I don't know," Joe said, "you don't look like you've been too lucky. Anyway," he continued, "I followed them until they parked in front of Charlie Yee's place. They took you out of the car, pretended you were drunk and carried you inside. Then I didn't know what in the hell to do. I couldn't go in after you, those guys had rods. I drove around for a while until I spotted this alley and I decided to investigate to see if the place had a rear exit. Sure enough, it did. Even had Charlie Yee's name on the back door. I spotted this window where some light was coming through but it was just a little too high for me to see in. I tried the back door but it was locked so I looked around for something to stand on so I could look in.

"Well, here I was prowling around the alley and here comes a car. And who do you think was in the car?"

"Cops," I said, "that's easy."

"Cops," Joe repeated, "and it wasn't easy. They wanted to know what I was doing in the alley."

"What did you tell them?"

"I told them that I had a call to pick someone up and the address turned out to be this alley. I said that it was beginning to look like someone was playing a practical joke on me."

"Did they swallow that story?" I asked.

"All the way," Joe said. "They turned out to be a couple of nice Joes and the first thing you know we're talking about the Giants and the Forty-Niners and the weather and how much nooky I pick up in the cab. I thought they'd never leave."

"How long were they there?"

"A good fifteen or twenty minutes, maybe longer, but they finally left. So I scrounged around until I found this old box that I could stand on. I put it under the window, climbed up and looked in. I saw you pushing those crates against the wall so I figured you were ready to break out of there. Then I saw you hurry away and I saw the door open and those guys came in. I couldn't see much after that. There were some crates in the way."

"Then you missed the floor show," I said.

"Yeah," said Joe, "and I'm glad I did. I've got a kind of weak stomach. Anyway, I couldn't hang around there too long in case that patrol car came back so I beat it back to the street and decided to wait for you there. But I wasn't going to wait too long. I figured if you weren't out of there in a reasonable amount of time I was going to call the cops, murder rap or no murder rap. It's better you should be accused of a murder than the victim of one."

"I came as close to getting knocked off as I ever want to," I said.

"You can say that again."

"I don't mean this roughing up I got."

"What do you mean?"

"It was just a lucky break that I didn't have the key on me."

"The key?" Joe asked.

"Yeah," I said, "the one I showed you this afternoon."

"So that's what they were after. It must be pretty important at that. How did you manage to hide it?"

I said, "I didn't. I left it on the table at Paoli's."

"Is it still there?"

"I guess so."

"Do you want we should stop by now and pick it up?"

"There's no hurry," I said. "It'll keep. Besides, I feel safer without it. So far there's been two murders committed over it and I don't feel like becoming number three."

"So they beat you up to find out where you had the key?"

"That's about the size of it. They couldn't afford to kill me until they had it."

"How many were there, just the two of them?"

"Three, including Charlie, but he didn't stick around too much."

"Why don't you let me call the cops and tell them I saw these two hoods dragging a guy into Charlie Yee's place?"

"No good," I said.

"Why not?" asked Joe. "Those boys should be put on ice."

"They would just deny everything and it would be your word against theirs. No, we'll wait. They'll get taken care of one way or another."

"So what do you plan to do now?"

"First I want to get cleaned up and patched up. This shoulder hurts like the devil."

"Maybe I can help out there," said Joe.

"How do you mean?"

Joe said, "I was a corpsman in the Navy—I might be able to set your shoulder."

"That's terrific," I said.

"Don't get too happy yet," said Joe. "It's going to mean doing it without any sedatives and it's going to hurt like a bastard. If you think it's painful now, just wait."

I grinned. Joe looked at me in the mirror with a quizzical look on his face. "What's so damned funny?" he asked.

"After what I've just been through, you're worried about hurting me a little."

"I guess you know," said Joe, "that you won't be able to use that arm for quite a while."

"I'll still be able to get around, though," I said, "although I don't know how I'll ever be able to drive a car with one arm."

"You don't have to," Joe said quickly, "not as long as I'm around."

"Now, isn't that strange," I said, tongue in cheek, "but that's exactly what I had in mind."

In a few minutes we pulled up in front of Lorna's apartment house. Joe helped me out of the car and up to the front door as though I was a fragile old lady. I pushed Lorna's button and waited. In a minute there was an answering buzz on the front door and we went up.

Lorna was waiting with her door partially open. When we came close enough for her to recognize me she let out a gasp. "Tony, darling, what happened?"

"He got beat up, Miss," said Joe. "Can we bring him in and patch him up?"

"Of course," said Lorna throwing the door open. "Put him on the couch."

Joe led me to the couch and eased me down while Lorna hovered about not knowing quite what to do. Frankly, I was enjoying all the attention.

Joe took complete charge of the situation. "I'll need bandages, cotton, alcohol, iodine and a pair of tweezers. Do you have all that?"

Lorna nodded. "I don't have any iodine but I have merthiolate. Will that do?"

"Of course," Joe said.

"I'll get them right away."

I grabbed her with my good left arm before she could move away. "Joe says I'll need some sedation."

"But I don't have anything stronger than aspirin," she said.

"Yes, you do," I said, pulling her down toward me. "You've got something that will make me forget about pain completely."

"Oh, Tony," she said, as her mouth found mine, hungrily.

Joe cleared his throat—a little louder than was necessary. Lorna stood up, a little embarrassed, and left the room.

"Quite a dish," said Joe with admiration in his voice. "I'll bet she can cook, too."

"You don't know the half of it," I said with a wink.

Lorna returned with her arms full. "There," she said, "I think I've got everything. What can I do now?"

"You can fix me a nice stiff drink," I said.

Lorna looked at Joe for confirmation. Joe said, "A stiff one— he's going to need it."

"Incidentally," I said, "Lorna, may I present Mr. Joseph Pinsky, the Menninger of the Yellow Cab set."

"Listen to him," Joe said, grinning, "and he hasn't even had that drink yet."

While Lorna fixed the drink, Joe busied himself with the alcohol and the tweezers. He wiped away the dried blood on my face and started picking out little slivers of glass with the tweezers. I winced with pain when the alcohol hit the open cuts.

"I'm sorry," Joe said, "but we don't want to take a chance on infection setting in."

"Why not?" I asked innocently.

"Because it's dangerous. You could die from infection." Joe spoke to me in the same tone of voice he would employ explaining it to a little boy.

I smiled. "We wouldn't want that to happen, would we Joe?"

"Aw, cut it out," he said, "you're ribbing me again."

Lorna returned with the drink which I downed rapidly. I started feeling better almost at once.

"Okay, Joe," I said, "do your worst."

"Well," he said, "we might as well get it over with." He put down the alcohol-soaked cotton and the tweezers. "This is going to hurt," he warned.

"So stop reminding me," I said, "and get it over with."

He moved me around so that I was in a prone position. Then he placed his foot in my right armpit and started pulling on my right arm. He pulled and twisted and pulled some more. It wasn't pleasant. Lorna turned away. I felt the cold beads of perspiration popping out of my forehead. I tried to think of something pleasant. There wasn't anything pleasant to think about so I started hating. I thought about Pinky and how pleasant it would feel to grind my foot in his face. I thought about how pleasant it might be to hang Eddie up by his thumbs with the tips of his toes just clearing the floor. I thought about—

"There," said Joe with a grunt. "Now, that wasn't too bad, was it?"

"Nothing to it," I gasped. "Is it back in place?"

"I think so," he said, "how does it feel now?"

"It doesn't hurt so much," I said.

"Don't try to move it," Joe said, "just lie still. Lorna, do you have an old sheet we can tear up?"

"I'll get one," she said and left the room again. She returned almost immediately with a sheet.

"I'll need two or three long strips," Joe said.

"Why don't you tear off what you need," Lorna said, "while I finish tending to Tony's face."

"Yeah," I said, "and while you're at it, rummage around the kitchen and see what you can do about a pot of coffee."

"Okay," Joe said with a grin, "I can take a hint." He took the sheet and went to the kitchen.

Lorna began ministering to my face. "Tony, stop it," she said. She continued her work. "Tony, how do you expect me to fix you up if you keep doing that?" She picked up the tweezers and expertly removed a tiny piece of glass. She held it up for me to see. "Tony, you're impossible. If you don't stop it I'll break your other arm."

"Don't you like it?" I asked.

"It's not that," she said, "but I can't concentrate on what I'm doing."

"So who cares?" I said. "Come here." I drew her down to me as she moistened her lips and parted them slightly. She kissed me long and hard, then abruptly pulled away.

"What's the matter?" I asked, with half-opened eyes, "don't you like it?"

"That's just the trouble," she said, working on my face again. "I like it too much. One more kiss like that and I won't want you to go."

"You wouldn't have to do too much talking to convince me to stay."

"I know," she whispered, "but you'll have to leave soon."

"Why?" I demanded. "My business can wait."

"But mine can't," she said emphatically.

"What kind of business do you have?" I said, reaching around behind her and pinching her firm buttock.

"Never mind," she said, removing my hand, "but as much as I'd like to have you stay, you'll have to leave."

"Expecting someone else?"

She nodded.

"I might get jealous."

She said, "I'll just have to risk that."

"Who are you expecting?"

"Nobody you know."

"Maybe I'd like to stick around and meet him. Hell, I've still got one good arm—maybe I'll just punch him in the nose."

"How do you know it's a he?"

"Okay, then, maybe I'll punch her in the nose."

"Tony, you're impossible."

"No, I'm not—just highly improbable."

"My," she said, "for someone who has absorbed as much punishment as you have, you're certainly in great spirits."

"That's only the effect you have on me—only this and nothing more."

"That's fine, Mr. Poe, just remember to leave before there comes a rapping on the door."

"Oho," I said, "so you're expecting the Raven."

She grew serious and said quietly, "Perhaps I am."

Joe popped his head through the doorway. "I can't find the coffee pot."

"I'll do it," said Lorna, rising, "besides, it's probably safer in the kitchen, anyway."

"How's it coming?" asked Joe as he approached the couch.

"The patient is displaying amazing recuperative powers," Lorna laughed on her way to the kitchen.

"Now, let me see," said Joe with a professional tone as he examined my face from different angles. "As soon as that black eye fades and the swelling goes down and those cuts heal up, you'll be as good as new. That'll be a hundred and fifty dollars please."

I started reaching for my pocket when I remembered. "Those dirty bastards took my roll. I haven't even got cab fare."

Joe snapped his fingers. "I knew I forgot something. I forgot to put the flag down. Now I'll never know how much you owe me."

I grew serious. "Joe, you never will know how much I owe you or how much I appreciate—"

"Forget it," Joe said, becoming embarrassed. "I'd do it for any bum I found wandering on the streets. Now sit up so I can bandage that arm up."

I sat up and Joe gingerly removed my coat and my shirt. Then he folded my arm across my middle and bound it tightly in place. He worked silently and efficiently. When he finished, he stepped back to appraise his work.

"I wouldn't take any chances if I were you," he said. "I'd see a doctor as soon as possible."

"Coffee's ready," Lorna called from the kitchen. "Shall I bring it in there?"

"No," I called back, "we'll come and get it."

Joe helped me on with my shirt and coat and watched me closely as I arose. He stayed right by my side in the event I was weaker than I thought I was. The aroma of fresh coffee wafted in from the kitchen tantalizingly. I shut my eyes for a moment and pretended there was no half a million dollars and no murderer running around loose. Only three good friends about to enjoy a good cup of coffee.

While we had our coffee I brought Lorna and Joe up to date on everything that had happened since the last time I had seen each of them. Lorna shuddered when I described the brutal beating I had taken. When I finished talking we sipped our coffee in silence.

Finally, Lorna spoke. "Why don't you give it up, Tony? You can take the key to the police and tell them your story. I'm sure they'll believe you."

Joe concurred. "That's what you ought to do, Tony, no fooling. You came close to getting your ticket punched tonight but you were lucky. Maybe next time you won't be so lucky."

"What if the police don't choose to believe me? What if they think the whole story is a cover up? What do I say when they confront me with the evidence of my fingerprints in Peggy's apartment? How do I answer when they want to know why I've waited this long to come forward with the information when I've had the key in my possession all day?" I paused to let that sink in. "Do you want more?"

Lorna said, "I don't think the police are that narrow."

"She's right, Tony," Joe said. "They may take a dim view of you withholding evidence but the worst they can do is slap your wrists and tell you to be a good boy."

"I won't argue your logic," I said, "despite the fact that I may hold opposing views—so let's put it this way; this has evolved itself into a personal battle. I've been framed, slugged and beaten—I don't take that kind of treatment lying down—not from anybody. If I was to find out, say, that you, Lorna, lied to me or that you, Joe, doublecrossed me, I'd come after the both of you, despite all you've done for me and all you mean to me. Do I make myself clear?"

"I'm getting out of here," Joe cracked, "before you find out that I'm a member of the gang."

"That's a good idea," I said, "we'd better get going. Thanks for everything, sweetheart," I said to Lorna.

"You're welcome, darling," Lorna answered. "And, darling—"

"Yes?"

"Be careful. Please, be careful."

"Don't you worry about this lad."

We all went into the living room. Joe and I were nearly out the door when Lorna asked me to wait a minute. She disappeared into the bedroom and returned shortly with something in her hand.

"Here's another one to add to your collection," she said handing me a key.

"What does this one open?"

"It's the key to my heart," she said. "It will also open the front door."

CHAPTER THIRTEEN

"WHERE TO NOW?" Joe asked. "Do we go get the money?"

I settled back in the seat of Joe's cab. "We'll have to get the key first."

"Paoli's next stop," he said, revving the engine. After we were moving, he said, "You're sure a lucky guy."

"Lucky to be alive, you mean?"

"You know what I mean—that Lorna, she's tops."

"She sure is," I said, fondling the key she gave me. "I never thought I'd go overboard again, but I'm weakening."

We got to Paoli's and Joe parked the cab. "Do you want me to go in?" he asked.

"That wouldn't be a bad idea," I said, "considering the way I look. We were sitting in a booth on the mezzanine, in case they want to know."

"Gotcha," Joe said as he slid across the seat and out the door.

He was gone about five minutes. When he returned he had a big grin on his face. He got into the cab and waved the key in the air.

"Nothing to it," he said.

"What did you figure you'd have to do," I said, grabbing the key out of his hand, "shoot your way out of the joint?"

"Well, you can give me at least a little credit," said Joe, "I might have stuttered when I asked for the key."

I patted him on the head. "Nice work, faithful companion. Now, shall we go?"

"Sure," said Joe, starting the engine, "where to?"

"To the bus depot and a half a million bucks."

"Where do we go from there?"

"Las Vegas, Reno, Lake Tahoe—you name it—anywhere we can spend it in a hurry."

"How about San Quentin," said Joe, "they say the accommodations are divine and the view of the bay breathtaking."

"Capital idea, old sport," and we both laughed.

We joked all the way to the bus depot. Being with Joe, I was unable to remain grim for very long. He had an irrepressible sense of humor.

When we got to the bus depot I handed the key back to Joe. "You do the honors," I said. "Look for locker number twelve—and don't get any ideas about going South with the loot."

Joe took the key and stepped out of the cab. Before he slammed the door he grinned and said, "Are you sure you can trust me?"

While Joe was gone I tried to plan my next move. With the money in my possession I had powerful bait to smoke somebody out in the open. I felt certain that I could bring the case to an early and satisfactory solution. I reflected on the tremendous force a certain amount of money could exert on so many people. Whoever coined the phrase, "Money isn't everything," must have done it in the booby hatch. A guy could get along without it for a little while but over a long haul that green could come in pretty handy. Maybe those early philosophers deemed it unnecessary but I wondered, if this was true, why they spent so much time trying to justify their views.

I checked my watch. Joe had been gone a long time and I was beginning to wonder if he had run into any trouble. Despite the fact that I had known Joe for such a short period of time, I trusted him completely. Then I thought, if I trusted him so much why was it necessary to reassure myself that I trusted him so much?

While I toyed with that conundrum, Joe returned, his hands empty and his face crestfallen.

I felt an empty disappointment in the pit of my stomach. "What happened?" I demanded.

"Nothing," Joe said, "that's the trouble."

"What do you mean?"

"I mean I didn't find anything."

"The locker was empty? Someone beat us to it?"

"I don't know," Joe said, perplexed.

"What do you mean you don't know? The locker was empty or it wasn't? That should be simple enough to answer."

"Oh, it was empty, all right," Joe said, "but I don't get it."

"You don't get what?"

"You know how these lockers are set up?"

"Sure," I said, "when they're empty, they've got the keys in them. If you want to rent a locker you drop your coin in the slot and that releases the key."

"Exactly," said Joe. "This one was empty and it already had a key in it."

"But how could it," I asked, "if we've get the key right here?"

"Maybe someone had a duplicate made."

"That doesn't seem very likely. Are you sure you were looking at number twelve?"

"Positive," Joe said. "I checked and double checked. I even went through the whole bus depot to see if maybe there were two number twelves."

"Damn it," I said, "I felt sure—"

"Who told you this key fit a locker in the bus depot?"

"Shorty. He checked a catalogue and said that this key fits lockers of the type that you find in bus depots and—" Joe and I exchanged glances and grinned.

"I guess we're both stupid," he said as he started the engine.

It wasn't ten minutes later when he pulled to a stop in front of the Southern Pacific terminal at Third and Townsend.

"I'm going with you this time," I said.

"So you don't trust me?" he cracked.

"It isn't the principle of the thing," I said, "it's the money."

There was a rush of people coming out of the depot as we entered. Evidently, a train from Los Angeles had just arrived. Joe surveyed the crowd with a practiced eye.

"Look at all them juicy fares I have to pass up," he quipped.

"You're making me feel like a heel," I said. "I guess the only way I can square things with you is to split the loot."

"You mean you weren't going to?" Joe asked with an air of feigned surprise.

"Hell, no," I said. "What did you ever do for me except maybe save my life?"

"You've got a point there," he came back at me, "but it's on top of your head."

We located the lockers and began a search for number twelve.

"Here it is," Joe called out, almost immediately.

"Is this one empty, too?" I asked as I walked over to him.

"Doesn't seem to be," he said, "at least there's no key in it."

"Maybe our luck is changing, go ahead and open it."

Joe inserted the key in the lock but nothing happened. "I can't seem to get it open. Here, you try it."

I took the key from him and tried to open the locker. I didn't fare any better. "It seems to go in all right, but it won't open."

"What do we do now?"

"Damned if I know—yes, I do, too."

"What?"

"It's simple," I said. "I'll just call Shorty. He'll figure a way to open this thing up. Give me a dime, Joe."

"That does it!" Joe said, reaching into his pocket and bringing out a handful of change. "What are you going to want next?"

"I'll think of something," I said, extracting a dime from his outstretched palm. "Now where's a phone booth?"

"Right down there at the end of this row of lockers. You go on down and call and I'll keep my eye on this locker."

"What for?" I said, "it isn't going any place."

I stepped into the first empty phone booth and dialed Shorty's number. It rang three or four times before Shorty answered.

"Were you in bed?" I asked.

"No," he said, "I was just watching a good murder mystery on TV. Where are you anyway?"

"At the Southern Pacific depot, Third and Townsend. How soon can you get down here?"

"I can come right away. Why, what's up?"

"That key," I said, "the one that Cookie dropped in the pinball machine, it won't open the locker."

"Does it go in the lock all right?"

"Yes, but it won't open it up."

"Maybe you've got the wrong locker."

"I don't think so," I said, "there's only one number twelve."

"Yeah," he said, "but it might be the one in the bus depot."

"We tried that one already," I said, "and it had a key in it."

Joe was standing outside of the phone booth frantically trying to attract my attention.

Shorty said, "Okay, I'll leave right away."

"Wait a minute," I said, "hold on, I'll be right back." I pushed the door of the phone booth partially open. "What's up?"

"Some dame just came by and cleaned out the locker."

"What?"

"There was a big cardboard box in there. She just walked up, stuck a key in and opened it right up."

"Why didn't you stop her?"

"How could I stop her? She had a key. It fit. Obviously, it was her locker. What did you want me to do, hit her or something?"

I grew a bit irritated. "Well, you could have done something, at least delayed her until I had a chance to get there."

"I did do something," Joe said, "I pretended to bump into her and I knocked the box out of her hands. It spilled all over the floor. Created quite a scene."

"It must have," I said sarcastically, "a half a million bucks in greenbacks and you spill it on the floor of a busy train depot."

"Cool your ire, sire," Joe said lightly.

"This is no time for jokes," I snapped.

"Well, she wasn't laughing either," Joe said, "the box was full of dirty laundry."

I heard a loud squawking in the receiver of the telephone. I put it back up to my ear and heard Shorty saying, "What in the hell is going on over there?"

"Never mind coming down," I said. "False alarm." I explained to him what had happened.

"Well, if you need me for anything else, just call. It don't matter what time it is either, call me, you hear?"

"Thanks, Shorty, I appreciate it."

"That's okay," he said. "By the way, you don't happen to know where Wanda is, do you? Is she out doing something for you?"

"No," I said. "I haven't seen her all day, not since I left the place this morning. The only errand I had her do was bring my car to the Union Square Garage."

"I know about that," said Shorty. "I seen her after I got back from Cookie's apartment. I thought maybe she was doing something for you tonight."

"No, nothing." I said. "Why do you ask?"

"Oh, it's probably nothing," Shorty said, "but she told me she wasn't going anywhere tonight and now she doesn't answer her phone."

"Maybe she decided to go to a movie or something."

"Maybe," Shorty said, "although she told me she was going to stay home tonight in case you needed her for something. She was real worried about you and thought she might be able to help."

"I wouldn't worry," I told Shorty, "she probably stepped out for cigarettes or something."

"Yeah, that's probably what it is," said Shorty, but he didn't sound convinced. "I'll call her back in a little while."

"You do that," I said, and hung up.

The air of gaiety that existed between Joe and I prior to coming to the train depot, had vanished like cigarette smoke in front of a fan. We were both glum as we walked back to the cab. Not finding the money was a tremendous disappointment. We climbed into the cab and sat silently for a few minutes.

Joe finally said, "What do we do now?"

"Damned if I know. Here I thought I had an ace in the hole and it turns out to be a joker."

"Sometimes the joker is wild," Joe said hopefully.

"Maybe it is," I said, holding the key up, "but I've got to find another card to pair it up with."

"Have you got any ideas?"

I took out my cigarettes and offered one to Joe. "I'm up against a blank wall. Oh, well," I shrugged, "if I can't go through it I'll just have to find some way around." I lit my cigarette and stared down at the matchbook. I toyed with it idly. Suddenly, I remembered the name and address inside the cover.

I gave Joe the address and said, "Come on, let's go."

"Where are we going?" Joe asked as he started out.

"We are going to pay a call on a Harley Perkins."

"What in the hell is a Harley Perkins?" Joe asked, his spirits reviving with the promise of activity.

"That's what we're going to find out," I said. "So far today I've asked a lot of questions but I've received damned few answers. From now on it's going to be different."

"That's the old spirit," Joe said, "we're gonna crack this thing wide open—but I'll have to make a stop first."

"What for?"

Joe turned around and gave me an exaggerated wink. "You want this bird to sing don't you?"

I gave him a tentative, "Yes."

"Well, then," he said in mock seriousness, "we're gonna have to get some bird seed."

CHAPTER FOURTEEN

I DIDN'T KNOW what to expect when I confronted Harley Perkins but according to the dismal neighborhood in which he lived, I didn't expect too much. Joe pulled his cab into a shabby section of San Francisco that I didn't know existed. Maybe I'd always been too infatuated with the old gal by the Golden Gate to realize that she had her shoddy side, too.

San Francisco was many things to me—a gay woman drinking sparkling wine, a perennial ingenue with stars in her eyes, a sophisticated matron presiding over important social functions. But now I could see she was something else, too—a dirty, tired old whore.

Joe stopped the cab in front of a rambling old building that once might have been a mansion but through the years had grown old and lost its glitter. Its once proud verandahs were now sagging porches. It was a fragile old woman wrapping her bare arms around herself to ward off the cold of a bitter winter. I couldn't help thinking, as I sat there and looked at her, that she was an old house with a broken heart.

Joe was watching something else. "Did you see her?" he asked.

"Who?"

"I could have sworn—."

"What are you talking about?"

"The gal that just left the building."

I remembered seeing her out of the corner of my eye. "What about her?"

"Did you get a good look at her?"

"No," I said, "I was busy feeling sorry for a tired old lady."

"Where?" said Joe, looking around. "I didn't see any—"

"Never mind," I said. "Now what were you talking about?"

"The dame that left the building a minute ago."

"Well, what about her?"

"I'm probably wrong. The light's bad and she was keeping to the shadows."

"Get to the point, will you?"

"Okay," said Joe, "I just didn't want to hurt your feelings, but I could have sworn she looked like Lorna."

"Maybe she did look like Lorna. What of it?"

Joe looked directly at me. "She looked enough like Lorna to be her twin sister. Let's put it that way."

"I appreciate your concern," I said, levelly, "but I'm certain you must be mistaken. Lorna wouldn't be caught dead in place like this. You yourself said that the light was bad, and—"

"It wasn't that bad."

"I wish you would make up your mind."

"And I wish you would leave yours open."

"Meaning what?"

"Meaning that there have been an awful lot of coincidences connected with that gal."

"And that's all they are," I said, "coincidences. Now, shall we go up?"

I didn't feel like getting into an argument with Joe and that was precisely the direction we were heading. I realized that Joe had placed his job in jeopardy by acting as my private chauffeur and self-appointed bodyguard. I was far too indebted to him to turn on him but yet I couldn't help feeling a little indignant about his allusions to Lorna.

We walked up the creaking old steps until we reached the portico. The place looked more like a boardinghouse than an apartment house. There was only one mailbox which seemed to bear this out. I rang the bell and we waited. After what seemed an interminable period, the door was opened a crack by a wizened old man in undershirt and suspenders. He had thinning gray hair and squinted at us through glasses that had that "Woolworth" look.

"What is it?" he demanded in a squeaky voice.

"We'd like to see Harley Perkins."

"You friends of his?" he asked, opening the door a little more.

"We want to see him on a matter of business."

"I guess it's all right," he said, after first examining us closely. "C'mon in." We stepped inside the house and he pointed a crooked, bony finger to a staircase. "Right up those stairs and to your right. Second door." And having discharged his obligation, he sidled into the living room to our right where the only twentieth century piece of furniture in it was a television set.

Joe shuddered. "This place gives me the creeps."

We climbed the stairs, turned right and stopped at the second door. I knocked.

"That you, Mr. Jamieson?" came a voice from the other side of the door.

I said nothing but knocked again. The door opened and we looked into the frightened pinched face of Harley Perkins. He had a slight build and delicate facial features with a pallid, almost transparent, complexion. He looked familiar. I was sure I had seen him before.

"Yes, what is it?"

"We'd like to talk to you, Harley."

"What about?" His slender fingers were playing nervously on the edge of the door.

"May we come in?" He didn't answer but opened the door wide enough to permit us to enter. His room was as shabby as the rest of the house. Everything in it was old, but it was neat. He indicated a couple of rickety old chairs for us to sit on. He had to sit on the bed. There wasn't much else in the room except an old chiffonier and a table.

I didn't know where to start so I said, "This is Joe Pinksy." They shook hands solemnly. "And my name is Ceaser, Tony Ceaser." He started to extend his hand, withdrew it, then offered it again.

"I see you read the papers, Harley."

"Are you the one?" he asked nervously.

"I'm the one," I said, "but don't be alarmed. I never kill more than two people in one day. It takes too much out of me."

He smiled, wanly. "I thought I recognized you," he said.

"From my picture in the paper?"

"No," he said, "from Big Sam's."

When he mentioned Big Sam's, it all clicked into place and I knew then what direction my questioning would take. "You were one of Cookie's—friends, weren't you Harley?"

"At one time, one of his dearest friends."

"I thought I recognized you," I said. "If it'll make you feel any better, I didn't kill him. Somebody was trying to frame me and now I have to find who that somebody was. But I need help. Will you help me, Harley?"

"I'll do what I can," he said, "although I'm certain that I don't know anything that would help you."

"You let me be the judge of that. Now, then, did Cookie have any enemies that you know of?"

He shook his head. "Jacques, Cookie, that is, never did anything to antagonize anybody."

"You said that at one time he was one of your dearest friends. How long ago was that?"

"Up until a few weeks ago."

"What happened to change all that?"

"Nothing I did, believe me. We were very close friends, you might even say inseparable. We even discussed sharing an apartment." Joe gave me a knowing glance.

"What changed your plans?"

"Someone came between us."

"Who was it?"

"I don't know. Cookie never told me. He merely said I needn't call him anymore."

"Did you try to find out who it was?"

He lowered his eyes. "Yes, I was—well, I was hurt. Here we were planning to get this nice apartment and share expenses and all, and we even discussed how we were going to decorate the place and I had such marvelous ideas—"

"Yes," I said, "I understand. You were deeply disappointed."

"That's putting it mildly. If I could have found out who it was that came between us I would have scratched his eyes out."

"But you couldn't find out?"

"No, although I tried, heaven knows."

"What did you do?"

"I went to Big Sam's almost every night."

"What did Cookie have to say to that?"

"Nothing, he ignored me. Oh, I tell you, it was humiliating. But I felt that I just had to know. You know what I mean, don't you?"

I was beginning to find the whole conversation distasteful, but I had to carry it through. There might be some little insignificant detail that would fit into a now vacant slot.

"And you never spotted your rival?" I asked.

"Not once. I think they were meeting before Cookie came to work or after he was through."

"Was Cookie close to anyone at all, that you noticed?"

"Oh, he was nice enough to anyone that came into the place, but that was part of his job."

For the first time since we came in, Joe spoke. "Did you ever see a great big beautiful blonde come into the joint?" He avoided my eyes as I glared at him. Harley, if he noticed the by-play, ignored it.

"Oh, yes," he answered, "many times. Quite attractive, if you like the type."

I changed the subject. "Did Cookie ever indicate to you that his life was in danger?"

Harley shook his head slowly. "No, he never mentioned a word to me. I'm certain I'd have remembered if he did." He started chewing on his knuckles. "What a terrible thing," he said, shuddering.

"Well," I said, getting to my feet, "I guess that's about it."

"I'm sorry I couldn't help you," Harley said, "but I told you that I didn't know anything."

"You probably have helped," I said. "All I have to do is figure out how. You're sure there's nothing else? Something that Cookie might have let slip—that didn't mean anything to you at the time?"

I could see he was trying to think of something that might help me but he finally ended up shaking his head. "I'm just afraid I can't help you." He started to see us to the door. "Do you know when the funeral is going to be?"

"No," I said, "I don't."

"I want to send some flowers. He was crazy about dahlias. We were looking at some day before yesterday, and—"

"I thought you said that you broke up a few weeks ago?"

"That's right."

"Then what were you doing a day before yesterday?"

"Well, you see," he began. "Cookie doesn't have a car and I do. What I mean is, he didn't have a car. Funny, I can't get used to the idea that he's—that he's no longer with us."

"I understand," I said, "but what's this about a car?"

"A day before yesterday, he called me and asked if I would take him someplace. I was so thrilled that he called that I told him I'd be delighted to take him anywhere he wanted to go. You see, I thought it was just his way of wanting to make up."

"Yes," I said, "then what happened?"

"I drove to his apartment to pick him up. He was very nice and all but somehow he seemed distant, as though there was something weighing on his mind."

"He didn't tell you what it was?"

"Heavens, no, he hardly spoke to me at all. He thanked me for coming by, though."

"And that's all there was to it?"

"Yes," he said, "I was so disappointed, although I didn't show it. I just pretended to be gay and carefree, never letting on that my heart was simply breaking."

"Yes," I said, "well—" I wanted to get out of there. The guy was beginning to bug me. But he wasn't finished talking.

"I kept waiting and waiting for him to say something or give me some little sign of encouragement, but he hardly said a word all the way to the airport."

"The airport?" Joe and I said it almost simultaneously.

Harley was startled by our outburst. He looked at us from under raised eyebrows. "The airport," he said finally, "that's where I was taking him."

"Was he going on a trip?"

"That's what I thought when he brought the suitcase with him."

"What suitcase?"

"He was carrying a suitcase when he came down to the car, and—"

We didn't wait to hear the rest of it. Joe and I went flying down the stairs.

CHAPTER FIFTEEN

J OE WAS CHUCKLING. I was riding in the front seat with him and we were on our way to the San Francisco International Airport.

"What's so damn funny?"

"As a couple of detectives," he said, "we couldn't figure our way out of the men's room at Macy's."

"Heaven forbid," I said, "we should ever get trapped there."

"Quite a character, wasn't he?"

"You mean Harley? An interesting psychological study."

"Hoo, ha," said Joe, "look who's going highbrow."

I ignored his remark. "You could tell how painful it was for him to discuss his love life with us."

"What makes a guy act like that?"

"That's a good question. Some are like that from boyhood, others acquire it later on. I believe medical science is divided on what actually causes it."

"And guys like that," Joe said, "they don't enjoy being with a woman?"

"I believe some do, but most don't."

"Ahh," said Joe disgustedly, "they're all nuts."

"Let's put it this way," I said, "they're not normal. But believe it or not, some of the greatest artists and philosophers down through history have been homosexuals."

"No kidding?" Joe said. "Anybody I know?"

"Well, there was a fellow named Plato who had a pretty good case on his friend, Socrates."

"What else would you expect from a couple of Greeks?"

"It even goes farther back than that," I said. "The Egyptians had a couple of homosexual Gods."

"No wonder Moses wanted to get the hell out of there."

"I'm sure you've heard of a chap named Michelangelo?"

"Don't tell me that he—"

"That's right," I said.

"Hmmm," said Joe, "maybe there's something to it. Naw," he reconsidered, "you give me a dame with nice boobs and a nice behind—"

"If I had one, I sure as hell wouldn't give her to you."

Joe was silent for a minute. "What do you make of this business? Do you think Harley was telling us the truth?"

"I think that whatever he told us was the truth."

"Meaning that he didn't tell us everything?"

"That's just the feeling I got," I said, "but I could be wrong. At first I thought he was just being gabby, the way a woman is. You know how they'll run off at the mouth once you get them started—especially when they're discussing love affairs."

Joe said, "I know exactly what you mean. You ought to hear my wife carry on about the guy she was going with before she met me."

"But after thinking it over," I said, "and reviewing the conversation, I'm not so sure that was the case at all. I'm beginning to feel that he talked so much to keep us from asking questions."

Joe started slowing the cab. "You want to go back and see if we can get anything else out of him?"

"No," I said, "I don't think it would do any good. We'd have to know the right questions to ask and, frankly, I don't know what they are. If we find the money at the airport, let's be grateful for that much and let it go at that."

"Do you think he knew what was in that suitcase that Cookie was carrying?"

"No, I don't," I said, "but, then, neither do we—for sure. We're just assuming the money is in it. But I still don't understand what Cookie was doing with it."

"Is that so important?"

"It is to me. If I knew how and why he had the money, it might be the key to the whole situation. The thing that annoys me is that the answer must be simple."

"Maybe you're just stupid," Joe supplied.

"You could be right," I said.

"Tony—"

"Yes, Joe?"

"I want to apologize."

"What for?"

"For what I said about Lorna back there."

"Forget it," I said, "you weren't out of line."

"It's just that you've got me so worked up over this thing, I can't see straight."

"I told you to forget it. I'm the one who should be apologizing."

"What the hell for?"

"You're giving up an awful lot to help a guy you hardly know. I'll never forget you for this."

"Whoa," said Joe, "wait a minute—wait a cotton pickin' minute."

"What's the matter?" I said.

"Do you realize what we're beginning to sound like?"

"No, what?"

"Like Plato and Socrates."

"Don't be silly," I said, "I could never fall for an ugly bastard like you. Besides, you've probably got hairy legs."

We both laughed.

Joe turned off the freeway and onto the airport road. "Shall I park it and go in with you?"

"No, you'd better wait out front. I may want to get out of there in a hell of a hurry."

"How come?"

"I've been pretty lucky so far that no one has spotted me and called the cops. This can't go on forever. My puss is plastered all over the newspapers. With this wrinkled suit and bloodstained shirt, to say nothing of my arm and the bruises on my face, I'm bound to attract a little attention. And if someone looks too close and recognizes me, I've had it."

"Believe me," said Joe. "The way you look now, even your mother would have trouble recognizing you. And if she did, I doubt if she'd want to admit it."

"Do I look that bad?"

"Take my advice and don't enter any beauty contests. But all kidding aside, maybe you ought to wait in the cab and let me go in."

"Can't do it," I said.

"Why not?" Joe insisted. "It was all right for me to go alone in the bus depot, why not here?"

"I shouldn't have let you go in then. It's too risky. What if something should happen and you got caught with the stolen money? They wouldn't ask you any questions, they'd just haul you downtown and lock you up. If they couldn't pin anything else on you they'd get you for being an accessory or for receiving stolen goods."

"But what about you?"

"I'm in over my head now. The worst I can do is drown."

"Aw," said Joe. "I don't see why you're worrying so much. Nothing's going to happen."

I said, "We've done a lot of kidding around up until now, but this is serious business. If anything should happen, and it's always possible, I want you to deny knowing who I am. As far as you're concerned, I'm just a fare that you picked up."

"It's a little late for that, isn't it? Lorna knows who I am, not that she'd squeal, but so does Harley Perkins. I'm in this thing as deeply as you are and you're stuck with me. You'll just have to make the best of it."

The air terminal at the San Francisco International Airport is a huge and beautiful building. The airline ticket counters are on the main floor together with enormous seating space for waiting passengers and visitors, a lounge and restaurant. The ground floor contains the baggage department and another lounge and there is also a mezzanine and upper floors containing an elegant dining room and offices. There are two approaches to the building, one leading to the ground floor and a ramp to the main floor. I had Joe take the ramp to the ground floor entrance. He let me off and parked the cab in a temporary parking zone.

I was beginning to feel apprehensive. I couldn't pinpoint any particular reason why I should feel that way but I felt it down deep in my bowels. Maybe it was the realization of how enmeshed I had become in something that was really none of my business. If I had only gone about my own business that morning after the police had released me, I should be in the clear now. I could go get Lorna and take off for Carmel without a worry in the world.

Then the back of my head began smarting and I felt a dull ache in my nose and around my eyes. There was a throbbing in my right shoulder and a tender area where my right arm came in contact with my ribs.

Then I remembered what I was doing there and why I got involved. The apprehension began slipping away because something else was pushing it clean out of sight. That something was a cold clear hard hate—a hate that was concentrated on one man. Not on Pinky or Eddie or Charlie Yee, they didn't count—I could find them and take care of them. There was someone else I wanted to find first. I wasn't in this thing for any money or glory. There was just one thing I wanted—blood!

I passed a newsstand and caught a glimpse of my picture on the front page of a paper. I grinned—it wasn't a very good likeness.

Directly in front of me as I entered was the long baggage counter with signs above it at spaced intervals denoting the various airlines. It must have been between flights because the place was nearly empty. To my right and to my left, along the walls opposite the baggage counter, were two banks of lockers. I went to my left but the numbers on the lockers were too high. I doubled back in the other direction and followed the decreasing numbers. At last I came to number twelve.

It appeared innocent enough. There was nothing to indicate its sinister contents—for which three lives had been sacrificed. I stood there contemplating it for a minute as though it was a shrine and I had come to pay obeisance.

"Yes, sir, can I help you, sir?"

I turned around to stare into the eager grinning face of a red cap. His grin vanished abruptly and his eyes grew large as he got a good look at my disheveled clothes and my bruised and battered face.

"No, thanks," I said, "I can manage."

"Y-sir sir," he stammered as he backed away. He bumped into an insurance dispensing machine, bounced off, whirled around and walked away hastily.

I chuckled to myself. I thought I must really look a mess. I turned back to the locker and fished the key out of my pocket. I inserted it in the lock and turned it. It turned nice and easy and the door swung open. I guess I had been holding my breath because I let it out in a prolonged sigh. I reached in and pulled out a brown imitation leather suitcase. It was heavy and almost slipped to the floor. I eased it down to enable myself to get a better grip on the handle. As I bent down I happened to glance up to the other end of the near deserted baggage lobby. What I saw gave me a start.

The red cap who had tried to help me was talking to a cop. He wasn't only talking—he was gesticulating wildly in my direction. The cop nodded a few times and then started walking toward me. He was about as far from the exit, which was between us, as I was. If I headed for the door we would meet in front of it. I didn't know if the red cap had recognized me or he was merely concerned with my appearance but I couldn't afford to find out.

I looked around for another exit. Directly across from me at the end of the baggage counter was the stairway leading to the main floor. To the left of the first landing, a few steps up from the floor was the freight elevator.

I picked up the suitcase and headed for the stairway. I concentrated on walking with an elaborate casual air. It wasn't easy when all the fibers of my body were geared for flight, but I didn't dare show any signs of alarm—it would be a dead giveaway. I made the landing and pushed the button for the elevator. The door rolled back and I stepped in quickly, pushing the button for the main floor as I did. As soon as it started rising I pushed the emergency stop button and waited. I tried to judge how long it would take the cop to go up the stairs but the best I could do was guess and hope I didn't guess wrong. I counted silently and then started the elevator back down. The doors rolled open silently and I glanced out. There was no one in sight. I picked up the suitcase and headed for the exit—fast.

My impaired right arm and the suitcase banging against my side didn't make for speedy travel. I was about five feet away from the exit when I heard footsteps clattering down the stairs behind me. I tried to move faster but I slipped and almost fell. By the time I regained my balance the cop had made it to the bottom of the stairs. I threw a quick look back at him and saw that he had his gun drawn. I didn't wait to see what he intended doing with it. I lurched through the doorway but not before there was a resounding explosion that echoed through the vast baggage room like a roaring cannon.

There was a searing flash of pain in my right thigh and the impact of the bullet nearly knocked me off my feet. I made it outside and headed for the nearest cab. I knew that the next few seconds were going to be among the most important ones I'd spent all day. The cabbie saw me coming and reached behind him to open the back door for me.

I tumbled in, pulled the door shut and said, "The Fairmont, please." As he pulled away I saw the cop come running out of the baggage room. He waved his gun in the air and yelled something. A small crowd began gathering around him and somebody pointed in the direction of our moving cab. We drove past the spot Joe was parked and I kept my fingers crossed. Joe pulled out right behind us.

"By the way," I said, trying to sound casual, "how much do I owe you for the ride out here? My company is very strict about my expense account. They want me to keep an exact itemized list, and—"

"What are you talking about?" asked the cab driver, partially turning his head. "I didn't bring you out here."

I pretended surprise. "Why you're not the same cab driver! What happened to the other fellow?"

"Look, mister," said the driver impatiently. "I don't know what you're talking about but I sure as hell didn't bring you out here."

"Oh, my gosh," I said, "this is terrible. I took a cab out here from downtown and told the driver to wait for me while I went in for this suitcase. He had let me off just where you were parked and I assumed—Oh, this is terrible. I'll bet he thinks I did this on purpose to get out of paying him. Look, would you please take me back so I can square things up with him?"

The driver slowed his cab, muttering disgustedly.

"Wait a minute," I said, looking out of the back window. "I think that's him behind us."

The driver braked to a stop. Joe pulled in right behind him. I climbed out of the cab as Joe came running over. I winked at him and said, "Gee, I'm terribly sorry, but I mistook this cab for yours. I don't want you to think that I was trying to get away without paying you."

Joe caught on right away. He grabbed the suitcase out of my hand. "What else did you expect me to think? You tell me to wait and the next thing I know you're running out in another cab."

"I told you it was a mistake and I said I was sorry."

"Okay," Joe growled, heading back to his cab, "let's get going."

"Hey," yelled the other cabbie, "what about me?"

"I don't know what to do," I said in a bewildered voice. I reached into my pocket. "How much do I owe you for your trouble?"

"Ah-h, forget it," he said in complete disgust and drove off.

Joe shut his lights and drove fast. He didn't take the ramp back to the freeway but turned to the right on the old Bay-shore Hiway and drove past the old terminal building. Then he took a left and headed for the freeway again. He turned his lights back on before he entered the freeway. When he reached the San Bruno cut-off, he swung to the right and went up over the overpass. We passed through San Bruno and a few minutes later Joe pulled off the road.

I said, "Where in hell are we?"

Joe motioned toward the dark rolling hills to our right "National Cemetery," he said, "I don't think anyone will look for us here. What happened back there? I thought I heard a shot."

"You did," I said, "I caught a slug in my leg."

Joe leaned over the seat. "Why in hell didn't you say something?"

"I didn't have a chance."

"Is it bleeding bad?"

"It's bleeding, all right. My whole leg feels wet and sticky."

Joe got out of the cab and climbed into the back seat. "We've got to stop the bleeding right away, but what are we going to use for bandages?"

"How about the one that's holding my arm in place?"

"We'll have to do something, that's for sure, before you bleed to death."

"At least there's one consolation."

"What's that?"

"If I did bleed to death," I said, inclining my head toward the cemetery, "you wouldn't have far to take me."

Joe used part of my sling to bandage my leg. The blood soaked through almost as fast as he wrapped the bandage but he eventually managed to slow it down and then stop it by applying pressure.

"What's going to happen to you next?" he asked, when he finished.

"Oh, I don't know," I said, "what's left?"

"I don't think you ought to try and find out," he said. "You should be in a hospital."

"You know that's out of the question."

"At least, you should go to bed. You've lost a lot of blood and you've had some pretty severe shocks to your nervous system."

"Yes, Doctor Pinsky."

"You won't think it's so goddamn funny when you collapse."

"Look, Joe, I know what the score is, but I can't afford to lay down on the job now that I've got this," I said, patting the suitcase.

"You don't even know what's in it," he said.

"There's only one way to find out, let's open it."

Joe reached down and lifted the suitcase onto the back seat. He fumbled with the catches. "Seems to be stuck," he grunted. "No, I've got it now." He lifted the lid and turned on the dome light.

Neither one of us said anything, we just sat there and stared. What can you say when you've got a half a million bucks sitting in your lap?

CHAPTER SIXTEEN

"**B**EAUTIFUL, ISN'T IT?" Joe said running his fingers through the neatly packaged bundles of currency.

"Be careful," I said, "that stuff is hot."

Joe murmured, "Water, water everywhere, and not a drop to drink."

"Ain't it the truth," I said. "Better close it up before it gets the best of you. Money is a powerful stimulant—especially that much of it."

Joe closed the suitcase reluctantly. He shook his head. "I don't get it, I just don't get it."

"What's bothering you now?"

"You are. You go through hell and high water to get this. You get beat up, a dislocated shoulder, a slug in the leg and what for? A whole suitcase full of money you can't even buy a cup of coffee with. Who needs it?"

I grinned. "Joe, how much money do you make in a year?"

"Including tips?"

"Including tips."

"If you laid it all end to end," Joe said, calculating with his fingertips, "it would take me approximately a hundred years to make what's in this suitcase."

"Good," I said. "Now, supposing I was to say to you, 'Joe, it's all yours. A hundred years of earning power wrapped up in one neat little package.' What would you do?"

"Don't tempt me," he said, "I might slip a shiv in your back and head for parts unknown."

"Fine. Where would you go and what would you do? That's what I want to know. Now bear in mind, this dough is hot. You just can't walk into a bank and say, 'I want to open an account.'"

Joe scratched his head. "Well, I'd... I'd take the money and ... yeah—what would I do with it?"

"Exactly. There's enough money here to set a guy up for life. He'd never have to do a day's work again as long as he lived and as long as he lived he could have everything he wanted. But there's only one catch—how do you spend it without being caught?"

"Why, you get yourself a good lawyer and—hey, wait a minute. So that's what you're leading up to."

"Right. If anyone could figure a way to cash in, a sharp lawyer could. How many sharp lawyers can you name real quick?"

Joe came right back with the answer. "S. H. Bertram and I suppose you want to call on him?"

"Right."

"And I suppose you want to call on him now, not tomorrow and don't pass GO and collect the two hundred dollars?"

"Right, right, right."

"Okay," he sighed, "do you know where he lives?"

"Somewhere on Nob Hill, if my memory serves me correctly, but we'll have to look up his address in the phone book."

Joe got back into the front seat and started out. "You know," he said after we were rolling, "that was a slick maneuver you pulled off back at the airport."

"Thanks," I said, "but it was a matter of necessity. I didn't have much choice. I knew I couldn't make it down to where you were parked so I had to grab the nearest cab and pray that I got out of there before the cop showed up."

"You just made it, too. A few seconds longer and that's all she wrote. I saw you come running out and I couldn't figure out why you were getting into that other cab. Then I saw the cop."

"I would have used the other cab, anyway, as a blind. That's one of the things I had worked out in my mind in the event of trouble. Someone was sure to spot me and get the number of the cab. After that it would be a cinch for the cops to find me. This way, we caused a little confusion, and before they had a chance to get organized, we were miles away."

"I've got to hand it to you," Joe admitted, "you sure know how to use your head."

"Yeah," I said, "for a punching bag."

Joe drove back toward the city until he spotted a restaurant. He went in to use the phone book and came out with two paper cups filled with steaming black coffee. "Careful," he said, handing me one, "it's hot."

I sipped my coffee until it cooled and then I gulped it down. I felt a warm glow throughout my aching body. "Thanks, Joe," I said gratefully.

"Forget it, it's just part of the service."

Fifteen minutes later we pulled up in front of a swank apartment building on Nob Hill. Everything about the place reeked of money. I got out of the cab and told Joe to wait.

"I'd be careful if I was you."

"Don't worry," I said, "I will."

"Not up there," he said, "but you're leaving me with a sackfull of money. How do you know I'll be here when you get back?"

"Easy," I said, "I owe you cab fare."

I walked into the foyer of the apartment house and approached the desk. The night clerk, with an arrogant air, eyed me with suspicion. I could see he was bolstering himself for the unpleasant task of hustling me out of there. He sat behind the desk and didn't say a word, just looked down his nose at me. From where he was sitting, it wasn't easy.

Without any preamble I said, "I'd like to see Mr. Bertram."

"I'm sorry, sir," he said, with a sarcastic emphasis on, "sir," "but Mr. Bertram isn't seeing anyone."

"He'll see me."

"He left strict orders not to be disturbed—by anyone."

"Call him and tell him that the gentleman who was in his office this afternoon is here with a package for him."

He raised himself up slightly. "I don't see any package."

"Listen, you worm," I said grabbing him by the collar, "I've had as much of your smart lip as I'm gonna take. I'm in no mood for playing games unless it's 'bash the nose in' and you're it."

I released him and he shrunk away. He sat there, deflated, unable to make up his mind what to do. I shoved him toward the switchboard. "Move," I roared, giving him a bird's eye view of my bicuspids.

He moved. He plugged in a cord, talked briefly into the mouthpiece and turned back to me. "Fifth floor. Elevator's straight back."

"That's more like it," I grinned. I marveled at how easily the clerk had been cowed by a one-armed cripple as I strode to the elevator. The elevator was a self-service deal. I got in and punched number five. The apartment building was so plush that even the elevator had a thick carpet on the floor.

Apparently, the fifth floor contained only the living quarters of Bertram for when I got out of the elevator into a small vestibule, there was just one door. I pushed the button and heard the faint sound of chimes.

The door was opened by a rough looking character who was dressed like a butler but bulged like a bodyguard. He didn't say a word, he just stepped back to let me enter. When I was inside he said, "Mr. Bertram is expecting you. This way please."

I followed him into an oak-panelled library. Bertram, in a fancy silk dressing gown was sitting in an easy chair holding a large brandy snifter. There was an opened book face down on the table next to him.

"Pretty soft for some people," I said.

"I like to be comfortable. Would you care for a drink?" I nodded. "Brandy all right? It's a very fine, very old brandy. I have it specially imported from the south of France."

"Bourbon, if you've got it. The kind they sell south of Market Street is all right with me."

"Certainly," he said.

"And a little soda."

"Clifton," he said to the butler, "a bourbon and soda for Mr. Ceaser." Clifton disappeared.

"Nice playmate you've got there."

"I find his services invaluable."

"Let me see," I said, "ten, twelve years ago and the charge was reduced from first degree murder to involuntary manslaughter. George Henry Clifton."

"Your memory is rather remarkable, Mr. Ceasar. It was eleven years exactly." Clifton appeared with my drink and then left the room.

"The night clerk informed me that you have a package for me."

"I might have," I said. "It depends on what you have to trade for it."

"That would depend, I believe, on the value of your package."

"Look, if you want to play games, it's okay with me, I've got lots of time. But don't forget, I've got the marbles and if I don't like the way you play I'll pick them up and go home. It's been a long day and as you can see from my appearance, not a pleasant one. I'm tired and when I get tired I also get irritable." I swallowed my drink. "Your move."

"You have a nice business in North Beach—a nice, quiet business with few problems. You never should have left it."

"I haven't left it. It runs pretty good whether I'm there or not, and I can't see what—"

"You also have a very attractive and efficient secretary. I believe you're rather fond of her."

"Get to the point."

"I'm sure you wouldn't want anything to happen to her."

My stomach muscles tightened. "Like what?"

"Like any number of things."

"You wouldn't dare."

"Wouldn't dare what?" he asked innocently.

"You know damn well what."

"Aren't you jumping to conclusions?"

"I'm jumping in exactly the directions you want me to jump, but let me tell you this—if I find out she's had one hair on her head harmed, I'll kill you. And if you know anything at all about me, you know I don't make any idle threats."

"Evidently, you don't know very much about me. I don't get bluffed easily."

"I'm not bluffing."

"Besides, you don't appear to be in the best of physical condition. You're hardly in a position to be dictating any terms."

"I've got one good arm left, that's all I need to hold a gun."

"I think you're working yourself up needlessly. You came here to discuss some business, let's discuss it in an orderly and businesslike manner."

"I've changed my mind," I said, getting to my feet. "I don't do business with slimy snakes."

"Tut, tut, Mr. Ceaser, flattery will get you nowhere. Do you know why I've had so much success in the field of law? I learned long ago to control my emotions. When you lose your head you lose your sense of reason. That seems to be your problem right now. You're not thinking ahead. After you go rushing blindly out of here, then what? You won't know where to go, what to look for, whom to see. Obviously, you can't go to the police. After you've calmed down and your sense of reason returns, you'll realize that you have but one chance."

"And that is?"

"And that is, to come to an understanding with me."

I sat down. "What's your proposition?"

"I believe you have in your possession a certain article that doesn't belong to you. I propose a simple trade."

"Go on," I said.

"I'm all through. There's nothing complicated about what I've proposed. I'm sure the terms are fairly evident."

"What if I don't like your terms?"

"As I've taken great pains to point out to you, you're not in any position to bargain. You have to like my terms, you have no other choice."

"Now, that's were you've made a mistake. Maybe you can narrow things down to a simple conclusion in a court of law. This isn't a court of law so the rules are different. I can play as rough as I like without getting cited for contempt of court. Actually, the only contempt in this case is what I feel for you and your friends. So now, you'd better listen to me."

"A very pretty speech, 'full of sound and fury but signifying nothing.' "

I ignored his barb. "You mentioned before I couldn't go to the police. Why not? I used to be a cop and I had a pretty good record. They're not idiots, you know. If I take them the money and the facts I've acquired so far, how long do you think it'll take them to figure out the rest? And how do you think you'll enjoy practicing law from a cell in San Quentin?"

Bertram laughed. It was a low, derisive laugh. "I've been bluffed by experts, Mr. Ceaser. I see that you have, very judiciously, avoided any mention of the fate that might befall your secretary in the event you pursue that course."

"Go ahead and have her rubbed out," I said calmly. "I can always get another secretary. Yeah, she's a good kid and I feel a certain amount of affection for her, but I don't owe her anything." I was watching Bertram's face as I spoke. He still wore the same cynical smile but there was an indefinable change in the expression around his eyes.

I continued, "I'm a hard nut, shyster. I don't go much for that sentimental bull-crap. I lost all that when I lost my wife. Now, I don't give a shit." I got up and headed for the door. I was reaching for the door knob when he spoke.

"Mr. Ceaser, what is it that you want?"

I turned around slowly. "You know damn well what I want. I want Angel Face Lawrence."

"What about the money?" He was beginning to show a chink in his armor. I wanted to split it wide open.

"I don't give a hang about the money, it's all yours."

"How much time do I have to think it over?"

"Your time is up right now."

He got up. "Will you allow me to make one phone call?"

"Make it fast."

He left the room and closed the door behind him. I didn't like the way things were going. It seemed to me that he was just stalling for time and I was getting fidgety. I wanted to get out of there. At first I thought I had him bluffed, but now I wasn't too sure. He was gone a long time. I paced back and forth restlessly and kept glancing at my watch. I was just getting ready to leave when he opened the door. He didn't come into the room, he just held the door open.

"Good night, Mr. Ceaser."

I said, "What the hell?"

"Good night, Mr. Ceaser, our interview is at an end."

"But what about our deal?"

"It should be quite apparent to you. I don't choose to accept your terms."

"Okay," I said, striding through the doorway, "it's your neck."

He saw me to the front door. Clifton was nowhere in sight.

I said, "I guess you know where I'm heading now?"

"I couldn't care less." He closed the door.

I walked over to the elevator and punched the button furiously. Nothing happened. I kept my finger on it and watched the indicator. It remained stationary, showing that the elevator was as the main floor. Evidently, someone had used it and then left the door open. I cursed under my breath and headed for the stairs.

On my way down, I tried to figure out Bertram's sudden change of attitude. Then I cursed again and started taking the stairs two at a time. My wounded leg hurt every time I brought my weight down on it but I tried to ignore the pain. I was winded by the time I reached the main floor but I didn't stop to rest. I made the street and looked for the cab. I breathed a sigh of relief when I saw it parked in the same place and I could make out Joe's dark form in the front seat. I stopped to catch my breath, then continued on toward the cab.

Joe was slumped over the wheel. I smiled and thought that he must have fallen asleep. I walked around to shake him and then I stopped smiling. There was something unnatural about his position. His cap had fallen off and the hair on the side of his head was thickly matted. I touched it. It was wet and sticky and then I noticed the nasty gash. I felt for his pulse. I thanked God that he was still alive.

He moved a little and started groaning. I cursed my own stupidity for staying away so long. Then I glanced into the back seat but I knew I needn't bother looking. It was empty.

I stood there, indecisively, not knowing what to do. Somebody made up my mind for me. I felt a rush of air and then my head exploded into a million fragments of brightly burning flashes. Then the lights slowly dimmed and gently faded out.

CHAPTER SEVENTEEN

I T WAS DARK when I began to realize that I was conscious again. At first I thought that I was in the middle of another nightmare and when I gradually realized that I wasn't, I thought that maybe I was going blind from so many blows on the head. But as I became accustomed to the dark I could tell that I was in a small room. There was a sliver of light showing in the crack between the bottom of a door and the floor.

I was lying in a heap on the floor and I thought that this was beginning to get monotonous. My head felt as though it didn't belong to me but it ached as though it did. When I started to move there was a twinge in my shoulder and my leg felt numb. Unfortunately, it wasn't numb enough for it soon began throbbing and burning.

I fumbled around in my pocket until I found my cigarettes and matches. I stuck a cigarette in my mouth as I struggled to a sitting position. I pushed the cover of the match book back, bent one of the matches double, then worked the cover in behind it. I was able to light the match by rubbing the head on the striking edge with my thumb. I lit my cigarette and then held the match up to get a view of the room. I was so startled by what I saw that I almost burned myself.

There was a woman tied to a chair in the middle of the room. She had her back to me but I recognized her immediately.

"Wanda!" I gasped. She didn't answer me. I hurried over to her and I saw why. There was a gag in her mouth. I pulled it off.

"Oh, Tony," she cried, "what have they done to you?"

"Never mind me," I said, "are you all right?"

She bit her lower lip and nodded. "For a while I was afraid they were going to—" she shuddered—"they were so—so filthy."

I noticed for the first time that her clothing was torn. There was a rip in her blouse and I could see a broken strap hanging down from the top of her slip. She seldom wore anything beneath her slip, she didn't have to. The top half of her breasts were exposed and I could see some dark lines that looked like fingernail scratches.

I got around behind her and started working on the rope. It wasn't easy with one hand but as soon as I was able to free her hands she helped me with the rest of it. Then she was in my arms, sobbing.

"Oh, Tony, Tony, what's going to happen?"

"Do you know where we are?"

"No, I was blindfolded."

"How did you get here, anyway?"

"I was sitting home tonight waiting to hear from you. I thought maybe you'd need me for something, like this afternoon. Then I got a phone call."

"Who was it?"

"I don't know, I'd never heard the voice before."

"Man or woman?"

"Man."

"What did he say?"

"He said that if I ever wanted to see you alive again I would have to do exactly what he told me."

"And what did he tell you?"

"He told me to get in my car and drive to pier twenty-seven along the Embarcadero. He said I should park the car, get out and walk around the corner to the dock side. I should then face the wall and wait."

"Why didn't you call the police?"

"He warned me not to. He said that if I told anyone about it, I would never see you alive again."

"Then what happened?"

"I did exactly as I was told. I was scared to death, it was so spooky down by the docks."

"You poor kid," I said, kissing her hair. "You should have known it was just a trick."

"I thought about it," she said, "but I knew I had to go even if it was a trick. I couldn't take the chance that they were bluffing. If I didn't go and anything happened to you, I'd never be able to forgive myself."

I looked down into her face. "I didn't know you cared, angel."

She threw her arms around my neck and pulled my head down to hers. Her lips found mine and she kissed me long and hard. I could taste the salt from her tears.

"You'd better knock it off," I said, finally, "or I'll forget where I am."

For the first time, she noticed my arm. "What happened?" she asked in a startled voice.

"Dislocated shoulder," I said, "I'll tell you all about it later. But you'd better finish telling me what happened to you."

"I went to pier twenty-seven and parked the car. I got out and walked around to the dock side and stood facing the wall. In a few minutes somebody walked up behind me and said, 'Don't turn around.' Then I was blindfolded and brought here."

"What happened when you got here?"

She shuddered. I felt a tremor go through her whole body. "I don't even like to think about it."

"I know, baby, but I've got to know everything."

"They brought me into this room and they started questioning me."

"What kind of questions?"

"They wanted to know all about you; where you were, what you were doing, anything at all that I knew. By then I knew only one thing, that I had been tricked."

"Did you get a good look at them?"

"No, they never turned on any lights. There was only the little bit of light we have now."

"How many were there?"

"Two, at first, and then another one later."

"When did the other one show up?"

"When the first two started getting ideas."

"What kind of ideas?"

As dark as it was, I could tell she was blushing. "They were going to—one of them started ripping off my clothes. I was horrified. I wanted to die."

"Those dirty, rotten, slimy bastards," I muttered. "What did you do then?"

"I started screaming. That's when they put the gag in my mouth. But I guess the screaming was what saved me."

"How's that, did they lay off after that?"

"No, but they started arguing."

"What about?"

She blushed again. "They—they were arguing about who was going to be first. It was terrible."

"Then what happened?" I said, gritting my teeth.

"While they were arguing the door opened up and a voice wanted to know what the commotion was all about."

"Did you see who was talking?"

"No, he was behind me, but he had a peculiar voice."

"Peculiar, how?"

"I don't know exactly, but there was the faint trace of an accent, one I'd never heard before."

"Did it have an oriental sound?"

"It might have," she said, "but I can't be certain."

"Go ahead, what happened next?"

"Anyway, whoever it was wanted to know what was going on. The other two said that they were just trying to get me to talk. Then the voice said that would no longer be necessary. He told them to tie me up in a hurry, that he had a job for them to do."

"So they tied you up and left you here. How long were they gone?"

"I have no way of knowing, but it seemed like a long time. After a while, they came back in here and they were carrying something that they dumped on the floor. It turned out to be you. Now, what happened to you?"

I brought her up to date on everything that had happened. She listened intently, recoiling slightly when I got to the gory parts. She touched the bruised parts of my face and then kissed it tenderly.

When I finished, she said, "That's what Bertram must have been doing when he left the room. He must have called over here and told them that you were in his apartment."

"That's the way it looks," I said, "and he must have sent Clifton downstairs to slug Joe and get the money. What a damn fool I was. I should have known better. Oh, well, no use crying over spilt milk. We've got to figure a way to get out of here."

"But how?"

"I don't know. It would help if I knew where we were." Then, suddenly, I knew. I wondered why I hadn't noticed sooner the distant fragrance of orange blossoms. I looked around the room. There was only one door and no windows. There was a small skylight but it was up so high that it couldn't possibly afford an avenue of escape.

"The door," Wanda whispered, suddenly.

I whirled around to face the door but I saw nothing. "What about the door?"

"I don't remember hearing them lock it."

"What?"

"I remember hearing them open and close it but I never heard the sound of a key going in or of the lock turning."

I went to the door and turned the knob slowly and carefully. Then I pulled gently and the door moved inward. I motioned for Wanda to follow me. We stepped out into a hallway. The room we were in was at the end of the hallway so we had only one direction to follow. After about ten feet it turned abruptly to the left. Fifteen or twenty feet ahead, on the right, light was streaming out of an open doorway. I motioned for Wanda to wait while I crept up to investigate.

As I approached the doorway I heard voices. Cautiously, I peered around the edge of the door jamb. I was looking into the same room where I had been held captive earlier that day. Eddie and Pinky were busily engaged doing something on the table. I couldn't see what they were doing.

I crept back to where Wanda was waiting and led her back into the room we had been in. When we were safely inside, I said, "No wonder they didn't lock this door. They didn't have to. The only way out is right past the room they're working in and they'd spot us in a minute if we tried to sneak by."

"What are we going to do?" Wanda asked.

"Damned if I know, but we've got to do something. It's a cinch they're not going to let us go when they finish whatever it is they're doing. We know too much."

"What will they do with us?"

"You'd better not think about it."

"Oh, Tony, I'm scared."

"Now, now," I said, encircling her with my good arm, "I'll think of something."

"But you've only got one arm and they've got guns."

"I know," I said, "but I'm smarter than they are." I laughed.

"What's so funny?"

"That last crack I made. I'm so smart that I did all the dirty work for them, let them kick the living daylights out of me and then I deliver the money right to their doorstep. And to top it all off I haven't got a prayer of finding Angel Face Lawrence now. Now that they've got the money, Angel Face, acting on the advice of the estimable S. H. Bertram, can clear out for parts unknown. Tomorrow, my body will show up somewhere, a suicide. There'll be a note explaining how I killed Cookie and Peggy and I wouldn't be surprised if I was the one who was in on the armored car robbery and killed the guard. What a boob! What a prize patsy I've turned out to be. I have now qualified for idiot of the year. Nobody can ever top this one."

Wanda cried, "Stop it."

"I'm sorry," I said, "I really am. But not for myself. I don't care what happens to me because no matter what happens, I've asked for it. But now, I'm responsible for putting your life in danger."

"Stop chastising yourself, it isn't your fault. You did what you thought was right and what seemed to be the only thing you could do. I'm the one who's a boob for falling for that telephone call."

"What is this, a mutual recrimination society? Let's knock off the chatter. I've got to think. Help me with a cigarette, will you?"

I took the pack out and Wanda extracted a cigarette which she inserted between my lips. I handed her the matches and she lit my cigarette, almost burning her fingers. She dropped the lit match hastily.

"Careful," I said, "or you'll burn the joint down." I took a couple of healthy drags on the cigarette as a plan began forming in my mind. "Why not?" I said aloud.

"Why not what?"

"Why not burn the joint down?"

"But what good will that do?"

"You'll see. Help me look around for something that'll burn fast." We made a search of the room. It was empty except for the chair and the rope that Wanda had been tied with.

I said, "Take your skirt off."

"What?"

"You heard me, take your skirt off."

"But Tony, do you think this is the proper time—"

"Oh, for Crissake." She was fumbling with the catches. I grabbed the skirt around her waist and ripped it off. I made a pile on the floor of her skirt and the rope. I laid the chair down with the legs of the chair on top of the pile. "Now, light it," I said.

While Wanda lit the fire I opened the door all the way. In a matter of seconds there was a roaring blaze. I grabbed the top of the chair and said, "Come on." We went back up the hallway until we reached the open doorway. I stepped in front of it and threw the flaming chair into the room. I reached in and pulled the door shut. Eddie and Pinky had been tripping over themselves in startled confusion.

I grabbed Wanda's hand and started up the hallway to the front of the store. It was dark and I didn't see him until we were almost on top of him. Then I couldn't see anything else. His great girth filled the entire passageway. I stopped short and dropped Wanda's hand. I lowered my head and charged. When I hit it was like hitting a big, soft pillow. My head sunk in up to my ears and I bounced back. Charlie didn't budge an inch. He just stood there blinking down at me.

Behind us I heard the door opening and footsteps running toward us. We were trapped.

Charlie hurled a string of Oriental curses at Pinky and Eddie and then said in English, "You fools, you blundering idiotic fools. Can I not trust you with even the simplest of duties? Were it not for me they would have escaped and had the police here."

"What did you expect us to do?" whined Pinky. "There's no lock on that door."

"Then put them in a room where there is a lock. Must I tell you every move you must make?"

"Look, Charlie," I said, "you've got the money, you've got me, why can't you let her go?"

"The answer to that should be rather obvious. She has seen and heard too much."

"What are you going to do with us?"

"The answer to that should be rather obvious, also."

"Suppose I offer to make you a deal?"

"It would seem to me that you've lost most of you bargaining power. Since you have nothing to offer, I am afraid there is no deal possible."

"Oh, but there is," I said quickly. "I have a great deal to offer, much more than you think. Look," I said, talking rapidly, "I've found out an awful lot in my snooping around and I did it running from your goons and the cops at the same time."

"It seems to me that you are merely tightening the noose that is already around your neck."

"You're missing the point."

"Which is?"

"Which is simply this—if I was able to do all this under a severe handicap, how long do you think it will take the police to do the same thing and more? There's nobody standing in their way and they've got the best crime detection methods available."

Eddie interrupted my speech. "Aw, what do you want to listen to this crap for, boss?"

Charlie snapped, "Quiet. Continue, Mr. Ceasar. I'm not quite certain that I follow your meaning but what you say has merit. Just what is it that you are proposing?"

"I'll take the police off your neck for good if you'll release Wanda."

"How do you propose to do this?"

"I'm not naive, Charlie. I know what's going to happen to me. Think of how it would simplify things for you if I left a suicide note confessing everything. Captain Coletti is convinced I'm guilty anyway, this would be all he would need to close the file."

Wanda, who had been listening intently, let out a horrified gasp. "Oh, no, Tony, I can't let you do it."

"Shut up," I snapped. "What do you say, Charlie?"

"You have just outlined the plan I had in mind, precisely."

"But with one major exception. The police would never fall for the phony forgery you would have to prepare but they'd have to believe it if it was in my own handwriting. And don't forget, since I was once on the force, they've got samples of my hand-writing on official documents."

"But what assurance can you give that once we release the young lady she won't go running to the police?"

"You don't need any assurance, you've got a smart lawyer. It would be a simple case of her word against yours and my confession would be there to back you up. Well, what do you say? Is it a deal?"

"I shall give it some consideration."

"How much consideration?"

"I'll inform you when I've reached a decision."

"I want an answer fast."

Charlie showed me a mouthful of yellow teeth. "I shouldn't think that you would be in such a hurry to get where you are going."

"Why not? At least it'll be peaceful there. Do we have a deal or would you rather take your chances with the police."

"I shall inform you of my decision when I have reached it. Take them away and this time find a door with a lock on it."

Pinky and Eddie herded us back down the corridor to a room that was opposite the storeroom and a few feet past it. They shoved us inside, slammed and locked the door.

After a cursory examination of the room, I said, "At least the accommodations are better. Let's sit down and be comfortable." I led Wanda to a studio couch that was against one wall.

"Tony, you're not going through with it."

"I don't have much choice, do I?"

"I won't let you do it."

"I've had a gang of goons and half the police force trying to stop me these last twenty-four hours. What do you expect to do?"

"I'll refuse to leave you."

"Do you think you'll have any choice? Wise up, baby, I'm really not that noble."

"What do you mean?"

"I've gotten away from these creeps before, I can do it again. But with you around it's twice as tough."

"I'm sorry."

"Don't apologize, it isn't your fault."

"Do you think Charlie will go for your deal?"

"He's already gone for it."

"But I thought—"

"That he wants to think it over? All he wants to think over is a plan to get me to write the confession without releasing you. He knows that whatever I told him was the truth. I don't think that Mac and his boys have exactly been sitting on their duffs. I just had a head start on them because of the key."

"But why are they keeping us here? If they intend doing something with us, why aren't they doing it now?"

"That's a good question," I said. "I think that the answer is in the storeroom."

"The storeroom?"

"Pinky and Eddie were very busy in there. Damn it, I wish I could have seen what they were doing. But whatever it is, it's important enough to finish that before they think of finishing us."

Wanda placed her hand on my arm. "Tell me the truth, Tony."

"Of course, baby what is it?"

"Do we have a chance, or is it really hopeless. You can tell me—I can take it."

"Sure, we've got a chance," I said, putting my arm around her. "We've got a darn good chance. I didn't want to tell you this because I didn't want to raise any false hopes in case it doesn't work out—"

"Tell me what?"

"I've got a secret weapon."

"What is it?"

"It's called a Joe Pinsky."

"Oh, Tony, how can you joke at a time like this?"

"It's no joke, baby. Joe Pinsky is the cab driver that's been ferrying me around all night."

"But I don't understand—?"

"He knows about as much as I do. Whoever slugged him must have thought that he was just an innocent cab driver who didn't know what was going on. When Joe comes to, he'll put two and two together and my bet is he'll go right to McGovern."

"Do you really think he will?"

"I hope he will."

"What if he doesn't?"

"Don't think about it."

She nestled her head on my shoulder. I kissed her forehead and she snuggled closer. "Tony?"

"Yes?"

"Do you like me?"

"Of course I like you."

"You know what I mean."

"You're talking just like a woman. What do you mean?"

"I mean, do you really like me?"

"I told you I do. What's this all about?"

"You always kid me so much I don't know when you're serious."

"Believe me, I never felt less like kidding in my life."

"I'm glad," she said, "it will make things easier."

"How?"

"In case—in case something happens. It will be good to know that someone cares."

I tilted her head back so that I could look into her pretty little face. "You're a funny one."

"I know," she said, fluffing her hair. "I'll bet I look a mess, and I don't even have any make-up on."

"I don't mean that way. As long as you've worked for me I've been making passes at you and I've never gotten anywhere. Now, all of a sudden, when I don't even know if I'll be alive tomorrow, you want to know if I like you."

"What's so funny about that? Women are a little different than men are."

"Thank God for small favors."

"I don't mean that way. We're much more sentimental. Little things mean a great deal to us. We're flattered, sure, when men make passes at us, but we know it doesn't mean anything. That's why it's important to know that you do like me, even a little, and not because I've got nice legs or—"

"You do?" I said with mock surprise. I looked down at her lovely tapered ankles and then ran my eyes over well-moulded calves and on up to her rounded thighs which her slip could only half conceal. "By golly, you do," I said as she, self-consciously, tried to pull her slip down. "Funny, I never noticed them before."

"Oh, Tony, there you go again."

"Does this look like I'm kidding?" I put my hand behind her head and brought it toward me until my lips were barely touching hers. I brushed her lips with mine in a tantalizing, feathery kiss and then I crushed her to me. She responded hungrily with her warm, moist mouth as she threw her arms around me and held me as tightly as she could. She pressed her body against mine and I could feel her heart beating beneath her filmy slip.

"Oh, Tony," she moaned softly, "I don't care what happens when you kiss me like that. Do you think I'm terrible?"

"No," I said, nibbling on the soft lobe of her ear, "I think you're wonderful. But then, I've always thought so."

"Then why haven't you ever told me?"

"I think you know the reason. I just never wanted to get involved."

"But you've been involved with other women. Don't try to deny that."

"I wouldn't think of denying it. But you're not that kind of woman."

"Don't be so damned sure." Her eyes flashed with a moment's anger and defiance. I was beginning to feel weak and hard and eager, all at the same time.

This was a new-found Wanda!

The studio couch groaned with our weight as I guided her down, then helped her slip out of her remaining clothes. The whiteness of her lovely body glowed softly in the half-darkened room.

I rose and stood over her for a brief moment, relishing her beauty, her desirability, then sank slowly into her waiting arms.

She curled her limbs around me, pulling me to her with a recklessness born of long waiting.

Her movements matched mine with a fierceness I had never expected from gentle Wanda.

"Oh, darling, darling! Oh, how good!" she moaned at last, her body convulsing with animal pleasure.

It was minutes later when she spoke again.

"Do you still respect me, Tony?" she asked softly, as we dressed.

"Certainly," I said.

"Damn it," she said, and I looked at her to see if she was joking or being serious. I didn't have the chance to find out.

We heard pounding footsteps, the sound of a key in the door and then the door burst open. Pinky and Eddie came charging in. They placed us back to back and started winding rope around us.

I started to say, "What the hell is going—" but I didn't have a chance to finish as one of them jammed a gag in my mouth. When they had us completely trussed up, they rolled, pushed and shoved us under the couch. Between the gag and my swollen nose I almost choked from the dust and musty odor.

Then I heard sounds of confusion out in the corridor and I knew what was happening. Joe had gone to the police and they were here now. I thought it would be just a matter of minutes until they found us and released us and this whole horrible nightmare would be over. Even if they didn't find us immediately, they would surely find the money. And finding the money, they would take the joint apart because they would know I wouldn't be far behind.

I heard footsteps pounding up and down the corridor interspersed with muffled conversation. I hoped that Wanda understood what was happening so she wouldn't be frightened by the rough treatment we had received. I heard someone shout, "In here," and I thought I recognized Joe's voice. Then it sounded like everyone was congregating in the storeroom.

Now, I thought, it won't be too long. They'll find the money and it will be all over. I was almost beginning to regret the police interference. It meant that Pinky and Eddie would be locked up safe without giving me a chance to get back at them. I heard the sounds of heavy objects being dragged across the floor as the police were evidently moving the packing cases in their search for the money.

It was then that I began getting worried. I had been sure that Pinky and Eddie were doing something with the money when they were working around the table. If that was true, why was it necessary to move all the packing cases? Then I thought that the goons may have had some warning that the police were coming and hid the money.

I waited what seemed like a long, long time before I finally heard footsteps approaching our room. They stopped outside the door and I thought I recognized Mac's voice saying, "What's in here?"

"Just an empty room," said Charlie opening the door, "as you can easily see."

A beam of light swung rapidly around the room, I heard Joe Pinsky's voice. "I could have sworn we'd find him here. This is the place they had him earlier tonight."

"You are obviously mistaken," Charlie said, "this is a legitimate business establishment."

"He's crazy," Joe said. "I stood on a box outside that window in the storeroom and I seen Tony with my own two eyes."

"Well, he doesn't seem to be here now," said Mac.

I tried to beat my feet on the floor or make some other kind of noise but it was useless. I couldn't move. I heard the door close and the sound of voices and footsteps retreated until there was nothing but silence.

I felt Wanda's body convulse with sobs but I was helpless even to comfort her. Comfort her—hell, I felt like joining her.

CHAPTER EIGHTEEN

AFTER ALL THE CONFUSION died down, Pinky and Eddie dragged us out and untied us.

"Thought you were gonna get rescued, didn't you, little man?" Pinky said with a sneer.

"I wonder how tough you'd talk if you didn't have a gun." I said. "It's funny how a rod can make a yellow livered punk so brave."

Pinky advanced toward me menacingly. Before he reached me I said, "You'd better not pick on me, I've still got one good arm. Why don't you beat up on Wanda, she'd be a better match for you."

Pinky grew livid. His pimples stood out as purple blotches. He shook his finger in my face as Eddie held him back. "It's gonna be a pleasure," he said, "a friggin' pleasure to rub you out. You keep asking for it and asking for it and believe me, you're gonna get it."

"Okay, okay," Eddie interrupted impatiently, "we got no time to stand around yakking. Come on, let's go, Charlie's waiting for us and he don't like to be kept waiting."

We were escorted to Charlie's office only this time it didn't look like a fruit stand. His desk was cleared for action and there was nothing on it but a pen and a few sheets of paper.

I said, "I see you decided to take me up on my offer."

"We have little time, Mr. Ceaser. If you will be seated—"

"Whoa," I said, "not so fast. There's a couple of minor details we haven't ironed out yet."

"Don't let him pull anything on you, boss," said Pinky, "he's just stalling for time."

"That's one of the details," I said, "get that punk out of here."

"Pinky, you and Eddie wait outside."

"But, boss—"

"Out."

Pinky glared at me as he and Eddie left the room. "We'll be right outside the door," he muttered to no one in particular.

"Now, what is this about details? I am merely accepting your proposal."

"What about Wanda?"

"The young lady will be released, naturally."

"How naturally?"

"I do not follow your meaning."

"I want to know exactly when and how she will be released."

"As soon as you complete the confession."

"You're going to open the front door and let her walk out?"

Charlie laughed. "I hardly believe she is properly dressed for the street." Wanda clutched her blouse about her self-consciously.

I said, "You know what I mean. Let's not play any cute little games."

"I am afraid I still don't follow you."

"What guarantee do I have that she will be released when I write the confession?"

Charlie looked at me in amazement. "You have my word, what else do you need?"

"That's not good enough."

"The word of Charlie Yee is good enough for anyone."

"For anyone else, maybe, but not for me."

Charlie's eyes narrowed. "It seems to me that I should be the one dictating terms."

"Guess again. You're giving me nothing except a passport to Hades. I'm giving you carte blanche to a half a million dollars. If you intend killing the both of us then go ahead and do it and

suffer the consequences. But if you don't want to suffer the consequences, you'll do things my way."

"And what is your way?"

"I want Wanda driven to pier twenty-seven where she left her
car and I want to see her get into her car and drive away."

"Then what guarantee do I have that you will write the confession after she is released?"

"You won't need any, I'm going to write it now."

"Then what is all the fuss about?"

"Only this, I'm going to write it now but you're not going to
get it until I see her released."

"Aren't you being ridiculous? What will prevent us from taking the confession from you after it is written? You are hardly in
a position to prevent it."

"Do you have any firecrackers?"

Charlie looked at me quizzically. "If this is some kind of
joke—"

"It's no joke. Do you or don't you?"

"I believe I have some in the storeroom."

"I want a big one."

"Now?"

"Right now."

Charlie shrugged his shoulders and went to the door. He gave
some instructions to one of the boys and we waited. In a few minutes Eddie brought in a firecracker. Charlie turned it over in his
hand and then threw it on the desk. I sat down behind the desk.

"Shall we begin?" I said. I started writing. It was slow and
laborious work writing with my left hand. I hoped that Charlie
wouldn't notice the grim smile playing around my lips no more
than he would notice that I wasn't left-handed. The confession,
when I got through with it, would be worth no more to Charlie
than the half a million was worth to me.

"How's this for a beginning?" I said. "To whom it may concern: This thing has been weighing on my conscience for a long

time. I can't take it any more. I've decided to make a clean breast of things and then commit suicide. It's the only way I'll ever get any peace."

Charlie treated me to a smile. "Excellent," he beamed.

I wrote some more. Wanda was sitting in a chair disconsolately watching the floor. Charlie alternated between pacing the floor and leaning over the desk to watch my progress. A couple of dirty looks discouraged the latter practice so he confined himself to pacing restlessly. He wanted to hurry me but he didn't dare.

"How much extra are you going to get?" I asked him.

He blinked. "What for?"

"I know you're cutting the pot with Bertram and Angel Face Lawrence. How much bonus do you get for getting rid of me and procuring my confession?"

"Does it make any difference to you?"

"Certainly," I said, "I want to know how good a job to do."

"Do the very best you can."

"How's this so far?" I read, "—the only way I'll ever get any peace. This all began a couple of years ago. Since I was once on the police force there were certain things I knew about security measures so it was easy for me to plot the armored car hold-up. Everything went off without a hitch—even better than I expected. They caught my two confederates which was okay with me because it meant I wouldn't have to cut them in. Then they caught a poor fellow by the name of Alfred Lawrence who happened to be dressed the way I was. This was all fine with me because it meant I was in the clear completely.

"I had only one problem—disposing of the money. I managed to pass a few bills but it was a slow process. I didn't know what to do. I had a half a million bucks and nowhere to spend it. Then one day, I took someone into my confidence. It was Jacques Coquette, better known as 'Cookie," the piano player at Big Sam's bar. Cookie told me he had a plan to dispose of the money. I gave him the money and waited for him to do something. He kept putting me off and giving me excuses that it took a long time. After a while I began to suspect a double cross. I asked him for the money but he said he had it in a safe place. I finally discovered that it was in a locker at the airport and that he had the key."

"So, that's where it was," Charlie said.

"That's where it was," I repeated. "How do you like what I've written so far?"

"Magnificent," said Charlie, "but it is a shame."

"What's a shame?"

"All that great literary talent will soon be snuffed out."

"Well," I said philosophically, "you can't win 'em all."

"I'm glad that you are accepting your fate gracefully."

"Just what is my fate?"

"You mean you don't know?"

"Of course I know that I'm going to 'commit suicide,' but how?"

"Very simple. You will jump off of the Golden Gate Bridge. People do it every day."

"Some of them get caught."

"We do not intend taking any chances. We are going to drive your car to the parking lot on the north side of the bridge and leave it there with the suicide note in it."

"Then you're going to get me to jump?"

"Hardly. I don't think we would find you very cooperative in that respect and, as you pointed out, some people get caught."

"Then the only other alternative is to take me out in a boat and dump me in the bay."

"You are very astute, Mr. Ceaser. Now, if you will please continue. Time is growing short."

"What's the hurry?" I said. "I'm in no rush to go anywhere."

I continued writing. Things didn't look too good. Even if they didn't kill me before they dumped me overboard and I had two good arms, the odds were that I could never swim to safety through the treacherous undercurrents of San Francisco Bay. If

I was going to make good on another escape, it would have to be before we got to the boat. But it would have to be between pier twenty-seven, where they were supposed to release Wanda, and wherever they had the boat moored. That didn't leave me too much of an opportunity.

Pinky stuck his head into the room to see how things were coming. Charlie shooed him out, started to close the door, then decided to leave the room, himself. He was gone just a short time but it gave me an opportunity to make a quick search of his desk. The only thing of value I found was a long, tapering paper knife with an ornate ivory handle. I slipped it into my pocket. Wanda watched me in wide-eyed amazement. I winked at her and she attempted a half-hearted smile. Charlie returned and looked from Wanda to me suspiciously.

"Are you finished?" he asked.

"Almost," I said, "just a few more lines."

He grunted, sat down, and watched me warily, like a cat watching a mouse. I figured that I had nothing further to gain by delaying so I finished as rapidly as possible.

I started reading aloud. "—in a locker at the airport and that he had the key." Charlie snapped to attention and listened carefully to every word.

"By this time I figured Cookie was going to double cross me so I asked him for the key last night. He told me he didn't have it but I didn't believe him. I told him I didn't want to discuss things inside Big Sam's because someone might overhear us. I asked him to meet me out back. I went out through the front door and walked around to the back. Cookie must have expected trouble because he sneaked out the back door and hit me on the back of the head. His mistake was that he didn't knock me out. I was so infuriated that I grabbed him around the neck. Before I knew what happened, he was dead. I killed him the same way I killed the armored car guard. I searched him but he didn't have the key.

"Then I had a brilliant idea. Cookie had provided me with a good out. I put two bullets in him and then pretended that whoever had killed him had also slugged me first. The story was so good, even the police bought it. I still didn't have the key but I put two and two together and figured that Cookie must have given the key to someone and the only one Cookie had anything to do with was Peggy, the cocktail waitress. I went to her apartment the next morning but she wouldn't give me the key so I killed her, too. Then I searched her apartment and found the key.

"I've been living with one murder on my conscience for two years. Now, I have two more and it's too much. And the irony of the whole situation is that I still can't spend the money. I'm convinced the money has a curse on it, so I'm taking it to the bottom of the bay with me."

I finished reading and looked up at Charlie. "There it is, all tied up in a neat little package for you."

Charlie was overjoyed. "It is more than I expected. You have certainly lived up to your end of the bargain. Did you sign it?"

I held it up so that he could see my signature.

"There is just one more thing," he said.

"What's that?"

"Would you mind adding a postscript?"

"Why not? Anything to make you happy. What do you want me to say?"

"You can express it in your own words, but I want you to explain that you had an accident which incapacitated your right arm making it necessary to write the confession with your left hand."

"How do you know I'm not left-handed?"

Charlie merely smiled. I wrote.

When I finished I called Wanda to the desk. I told her to roll the confession around the firecracker leaving the wick sticking out. Then I had her light me a cigarette. Charlie watched me, fascinated.

"Okay, Charlie, call your goons in."

Charlie went to the door and beckoned Pinky and Eddie to enter. When everyone was in the room I said, "Now, Charlie, tell your boys what the score is in front of Wanda and me."

Charlie raised his eyebrows. "The score?"

"Tell them about our deal and how it's going to work."

Charlie turned to his boys. "Mr. Ceaser and myself have made a little business deal. He has written a confession in exchange for which I have guaranteed the release of the young lady."

Pinky said, "So she can go running to the cops? Are you crazy?"

"It will avail her of nothing to go to the police since Mr. Ceaser has confessed, taking full responsibility for all misdeeds. Now then, you see the confession rolled up in his hand. He will give it to you when you have released the young lady at pier twenty-seven. Is all that clear?"

Pinky said, "Why don't we cut out all this baloney and take it away from him?"

Charlie laughed. "Mr. Ceaser is quite clever, as you well know. He has a firecracker in the center of the confession. He also has a lighted cigarette. He has merely to put the two together and the confession will be blown to a thousand pieces. I needn't tell you that I want the confession returned to me intact."

Pinky still refused to believe the instructions. "You mean you're actually going through with this crazy deal?"

"Precisely," said Charlie, "now, be off."

"Not so fast," I said, "haven't you forgotten something?"

Charlie frowned. "I can't think of a thing."

"Well, I can," I said. "Remember, this is supposed to look like a suicide. Suicide by drowning, as a matter of fact. When they recover my body they'd better find water in my lungs or they may get very suspicious. And when the police get suspicious, they also get very nasty."

Charlie said, "And the point of all this?"

"Just this," I said, "tell your goons, especially the ugly one here," I pointed to Pinky, "that they don't have to weigh me down with lead to make sure I sink."

Charlie laughed. "Even in the face of death, you have an incredible sense of humor. Such a pity I can't keep you here to amuse me."

"Yeah," I said, "we've had loads of chuckles, but don't feel bad, I may come back to haunt you."

"Now, be off," Charlie said.

We started for the door. I stopped and turned toward Charlie. "Just one more thing. I'm sure you'll grant the condemned man a last request."

"It would be inhuman to refuse."

"Tell me," I said, "where in the hell *is* Angel Face Lawrence?"

"It is a pity," said Charlie, "that you will never know how close you came to finding him."

"You're not going to tell me?"

"If you will forgive me for being cryptic," he said, "I shall quote you a proverb. It will give you something to ponder other than your imminent fate. Possibly, in the moment of truth, before you perish, it will come to you."

"Okay," I said, "let's have it."

"It is a proverb of your country, I believe. It states simply, 'Sometimes, one cannot see the forest because of the trees.' "

"I'll think about it," I said, "the next time I run into a tree."

They had the car waiting out in the alley. Pinky got in behind the wheel and they made me get into the front seat beside him while Wanda got in the back with Eddie.

After the car was moving, Eddie said. "Don't get any smart ideas or the broad gets it."

I ignored him and turned to Wanda. "Listen, honey, I never got around to making a will. Will you see to it that Shorty takes over the business?"

She was rubbing tears out of her eyes as she nodded. She tried to talk but she couldn't seem to manage anything coherent.

I said, "Take it easy, sweetheart, it isn't as bad as all that."

Pinky couldn't resist the opening. "No," he said, "it's worse. But don't worry about him, I'll come around and take care of you."

This brought on a new wave of tears. "Don't pay any attention to the filthy rat," I said. "If he ever tries to bother you just call Mac."

Wanda finally managed to calm down enough to talk. "Tony, I'll never forget you."

"I hope you don't," I said, "but take my advice and find a nice quiet chicken plucker from Petaluma and settle down."

"For a guy who hasn't got long to live," said Pinky, "you sure talk awful brave."

"That's the difference between a man and a punk," I said.

"We'll see," he sneered, "when the time comes. You'll be begging for mercy on your hands and knees."

"Maybe nobody ever told you about me," I said, "but I die real hard. The trouble with a punk like you is, just because you've got no guts, you think no one else has."

"Keep talking, little man, because the more you talk, the more pleasure it's gonna give me when you get it."

I chuckled and watched Pinky's body stiffen. Eddie nervously lit a cigarette. "I wish we'd get this over with," he said, "it's been a long day."

"Getting a little jumpy?" I said. "What's the matter, haven't you ever knocked anyone off before?"

"Will you shut up?" he said.

"No, why should I? I'm enjoying myself watching you worms wiggle. You look a little pale, Eddie, maybe Pinky should stop the car so you can puke."

"I said knock it off."

Pinky said, "Don't let him shake you up."

"You can knock it off, too."

"Don't tell me what to do," Pinky said.

"You see," I said to Wanda, "they're so miserable they can't even stomach each other. No matter how tough a guy is, it's never easy for him to take someone else's life. When he's faced with the job, he notices funny things happening to himself; his hands start sweating, there's a lump in his throat that won't dissolve, there's an awful pounding in his chest where he knows his heart ought to be."

"God damn you," Eddie cursed, "knock it off."

I said calmly, "Don't get hysterical, not yet, anyway. Wait until you're through with me. When you push me off the boat I want you to be thinking of your mother. Think of how proud she'd be if she could see what you were doing."

Pinky said, "I got news for you, little man, my mother was a pig. Never drew a sober breath in her life. Drank herself right into the grave. Now, try something else and see where it'll get you."

"That's odd," I said.

"What's odd?"

"You said your mother was a pig. I would have sworn she was a mare."

"What kind of a crack is that?"

"Only a mare could give birth to a horse's ass like you."

There was no more conversation until we reached pier twenty-seven. Pinky rolled to a stop about fifty feet from Wanda's car.

"Get going, baby, and don't look back. Go right home and take a handful of sleeping pills."

"Good-bye, Tony," she said, and she got out of the car. As she started running, Pinky grabbed the confession out of my hand. I had been so intent watching Wanda that I was caught off guard.

Then I saw something that made my blood run cold. Eddie had his arm hanging out of the window and he was raising it slowly. There was a gun at the end of it and he was taking aim. I screamed a warning to Wanda and then I tried to go for Eddie. I didn't get very far. Pinky hit me a glancing blow on the head at the same time that I saw the orange flash and heard the explosion.

The blow didn't knock me out but it made me groggy. I thought I saw Wanda fall. Pinky gunned the engine and roared away.

CHAPTER NINETEEN

A FOGHORN MOANED sadly in the distance. I listened to its mournful cry as they hustled me onto the boat. My last chance for escape was seemingly swallowed up in the dense fog that enveloped us. They shoved me down into the cabin and locked the door. There were four bunks, two stacked on each side of the passageway. I crawled into one of the lower bunks and collapsed.

My leg was inflamed and there was a steady throbbing in my shoulder intensified by my inactivity. My face and head felt like raw hamburger and a nagging nausea settled in my stomach. I was getting to the point where I felt that death might be a welcome relief. I knew that if I shut my eyes I might never open them again and the temptation was an appealing one.

I heard the water lapping on the hull and then I felt a steady vibration as the engine started up. Soon the boat settled down in a steady rocking motion and we were underway.

I knew that if I passed out, I was finished so I tried to concentrate on keeping my eyes open and my mind occupied. The events of the past day whirled around me in jumbled confusion so I tried to sort them out. I knew that if I could solve Cookie's involvement in the mess I would have a key to the entire mystery. Somehow, I couldn't picture Cookie as the criminal type. It just didn't make sense. Then what other way could he be involved? An image of Harley Perkins floated into my subconscious mind and floated back out again. I saw myself standing in front of a tree that suddenly turned into—

I sat bolt upright as things suddenly began clicking into place. It was like hitting the right combination on a pinball machine. It was getting the right balls in the right holes. I had been floundering around, shooting aimlessly and trusting to luck rather than taking a scientific approach.

I fell back onto the bunk. What good was it all now? In a few minutes they would be coming after me and it would all be over. They? Both of them couldn't come. One of them would have to stay at the wheel. I felt for the paper knife. Maybe there was a chance. Even if it was only a slim chance it was better than giving up without a try. What the hell, the worst they could do was kill me and they had every intention of doing that anyway.

I fingered the paper knife. It didn't have much of an edge but it had a sharp point. I had one other thing working for me—the element of surprise. Many a military victory had been achieved with that simple expediency. I worked a plan out in my mind, step by step. My advantage would be brief. I would have but one opportunity to capitalize on it. I couldn't afford to fail.

I tried to relax and conserve my strength. There was something else I knew I should be thinking about. It bothered me, wouldn't let me rest. It swam beneath the surface of my subconscious mind, a tantalizing white form that wouldn't surface. Then Eddie opened the door and called something down to me and it popped up.

It popped up in the glare of a white rage and the image was Wanda running to her car and Eddie raising his gun. I felt the blood pounding in my temples as my stomach churned in an uncontrollable fury of hate.

Eddie clumped down the ladder with the heavy steps of an executioner. The first thing I saw was the gun, then his arm, then the rest of him. He stood over my bunk.

"Let's go," he said, "it's time."

I got up slowly, hiding the paper knife under my coat. I got to my feet and swayed uncertainly.

Eddie said. "What's the matter, wise guy, your knees turning to jelly? I thought you die real hard?"

"Are you religious, Eddie?"

He spat. "Hell, no."

"Then while I'm praying, I'll pray for your salvation as well as mine." I knelt down in front of him.

"Get him," he said, "the little big shot down on his knees. Pinky should be here to see this."

My head was in line with his belt. He stood there with a sneer on his face, the gun dangling limply at his side. He made an obvious display of enjoying my prostration. His enjoyment didn't last long. I got up slowly but my left hand moved fast as I buried the paper knife in his stomach. He didn't move. He stood there with a look of stunned surprise on his face. I pulled the knife out and drove it in again. He crumbled slowly, like a giant balloon with a small leak. His warm sticky blood covered my hand.

I stood over him breathing heavily conscious of nothing but the intense pounding of my heart. "That's for Wanda," I whispered, "you slimy son-of-a-bitch." But I didn't feel relieved or avenged—just weary.

I pried the gun out of his hand and stuck it in my pocket. Next came the hard job. I had to haul Eddie up the ladder. It was no easy chore. Eddie was no midget and the ladder was almost vertical. It would have been a tough job if both my arms were operative. With one out of commission it was virtually impossible. I could make only one step at a time before getting winded and I would have to stop and rest. I was afraid that I was taking far too much time and that Pinky might decide to come below and investigate.

I wasn't worried about having a showdown with Pinky because with the gun in my pocket we were on equal terms. But if I did manage to get him before he got me I'd be lost somewhere in the middle of the bay in a dense fog and I'd never find my way back. Worse yet, there was the possibility that I would inadvertently head out to sea if I tried to guide the boat.

I don't know how I did it but I finally managed to drag Eddie's body on deck.

Pinky called back from somewhere up forward. "That you Eddie? Christ, I thought you'd never come up. What in the hell took you so long?"

I couldn't risk imitating Eddie's voice. I said, "Pinky, you've got to listen to me. I want to make a deal."

Pinky laughed. "I'm busy. Make your deal with Eddie."

"I've been trying to talk to him, he won't listen. He won't even answer me."

"Now, isn't that a shame. What kind of a deal do you want to make?"

"Don't go through with this and I'll make it worth your while."

"Beg, little man, beg."

I didn't answer him right away, then I said, in a voice I hoped was full of humiliation. "All right, I'm begging."

For an answer I got a cackle. "What did I tell you, Eddie? He talked real big, didn't he? Now listen to him. Is he down on his knees? How much is it worth to you, little man, to keep on living?"

"I'll give you ten thousand dollars."

"Chicken feed."

"I'll make it twenty."

"Where will you get that kind of dough?"

"I've got some of it, I'll raise the rest of it. I'll sell my business, my car, everything I own."

"Make it fifty grand and you've got a deal."

"Fifty grand!" I said. "I could never raise that kind of dough."

"Now isn't that a shame? I guess we got no choice then, huh Eddie?"

"No, no," I screamed, "don't do it."

"Hurry up, Eddie, that creep is making me sick. I can't stand a cry baby and, besides, we've gotta head back."

I took the gun out of my pocket and hit the dead Eddie on the head. The sound carried through the fog with a hollow echo. I pushed his body overboard.

"How did you like that?" Pinky called out. "He was the guy who never got scared. Just goes to show you. Boy, I hope I can find my way back in this lousy fog."

I had to gamble to keep Pinky from getting suspicious about Eddie's silence. I mumbled something about going below, then I opened the door to the cabin and slammed it shut.

I sat down on the deck and waited. I checked the gun to make sure the safety catch was off. The trip back seemed longer than the trip out. It always does. I could hear Pinky humming a tune. Once in a while I could see the glow of a cigarette which merely heightened my desire for one. I was getting cramped sitting in one position but I didn't dare move.

At last I saw the dim glow of lights which told me we were nearing shore. Pinky called out, "Eddie." He waited, then swore. "God damn him, sacking out and letting me do all the work."

We bumped into our berth and Pinky cut the engine. He secured a line forward, then came aft. He threw open the door to the cabin and called down, "Come on, let's get going."

"He won't answer you," I said calmly, "he's dead."

Pinky froze for an instant, then whirled around, his gun spitting flame. His shots went wild. I took careful aim and squeezed the trigger. My first shot got him but I pumped three more slugs into him before I was satisfied. The only reason I stopped was that the gun was empty.

I walked over to where he was sprawled on the deck and went through his pockets. I wanted two things, some small change for a phone call and the keys to the car.

I got off the boat and stopped only long enough to find her name on the hull. She was the "Laurie Jean." I found the car and drove until I found an outside phone booth near a service station that was closed. It wasn't easy driving with one arm but I managed.

I dialed police headquarters then looked at my watch. It was close to two o'clock in the morning, almost exactly twenty-four hours since this wild escapade began.

I asked for Mac and waited. I knew he'd be there. He was.

"Hello, buddy," I said.

"Tony, where in the hell are you? I've got half the force out looking for you."

"You can call them off," I said, "I'm not lost anymore. Look, there's no time to lose. Will you get an ambulance down to pier twenty-seven and—"

He cut me off. "That won't be necessary."

I choked up. "You mean—"

"I mean she's right here with me."

"But I saw her fall."

"She dropped to the ground when you yelled."

I let my breath out. "Thank God. Okay, listen—take a squad of men down to Charlie Yee's and pick up the money?"

"We've been there, remember? We couldn't find a damn thing. We turned the place upside down."

"That's because you just didn't know where to look. Did you see any canned shrimp while you were in the storeroom?"

"What the hell are you talking about?"

"They've got a canning machine there. That's what they were doing while they held Wanda and me captive—they were putting the money in cans and sealing it up."

Mac said, "I'll be damned! Now that you mention it, I did see a couple of cases of something on the table."

"When you finish with that you can send the meat wagon down to Yacht Harbor."

"What for?"

"You'll find a stiff on the 'Laurie Jean.' "

Mac said, "I thought there were two of them. Where's the other one?"

"You'll have to fish him out of the bay. If you check the records I think you'll find that the 'Laurie Jean' belongs to S. H. Bertram but I doubt if you'll be able to tie him in with this thing. He's too slick."

"Tony, I want you to come down to headquarters."

"What for?"

"I've still got a lot of questions."

"I haven't got all the answers yet. I've got most of them but there's one more thing."

"What's that?"

"Not what—who?"

"You mean Angel Face?"

"I don't mean your grandmother."

"Why don't you let us take care of him? After the way this thing has broken wide open, you're in the clear. Why don't you knock off. From what I hear you're in no shape to be walking around, let alone track down a killer."

I said, "The reports you've heard are highly exaggerated. I've got a few scratches, that's all."

"I know better. Joe Pinsky's here and he's told me the whole story."

"What in the hell is he doing there?"

"He's haunting me. I can't get rid of him. He's been bugging me to find you."

"You know why, don't you?"

"Why?"

"I owe him a cab fare."

Mac laughed. "You'd think he was your father the way he's been worrying."

I had a sudden thought. "Mac, wasn't there a reward for the recovery of the loot?"

"Yes," he said, "a pretty substantial one."

"Good, will you see to it that Joe gets it?"

"But why? It should go to you."

"I wouldn't be here now if it wasn't for him. Besides, he had as much to do with tracking it down as I did."

"Okay, I'll see what I can do. Now, what about you?"

"What about me?"

"Are you going home now?"

"No."

"Where are you going?"

"That's my business."

"Well, I'm making it my business."

"Good luck," I said and I hung up.

Mac was a good cop but sometimes he got too nosey.

CHAPTER TWENTY

THE FOG HUNG OVER the street like blankets on a clothesline. It was hard enough driving the car with two arms in a dense fog. This was impossible. I had to keep the side window open so I could stick my neck out and peer ahead. As I got further away from the water the fog thinned out a bit. Not much, but it was a help. I found the street I wanted and turned into it. I had to crawl along until I found the right building. There were no lights on in any of the upstairs rooms. At that time of the morning I didn't think there would be.

I used my key in the front door and rode the elevator up to the third floor. I was going to use my key again but thought better of it. I didn't want to frighten her. I punched the button and waited. In a few minutes there were sounds of movement and a faint glow of light under the door. Then she opened the door cautiously and squinted into the shadow that was hiding me.

"Tony!" she said at last. She was wearing a robe and rubbing the sleep out of her eyes but she didn't have a hair out of place. I couldn't see her face too distinctly for the light that was behind her provided her golden hair with a halo that framed her face in darkness.

"May I come in?"

"Of course." She flung the door open and stepped aside. I crossed over to the couch and sank into it wearily. She sat in a chair across from me. The room was illluminated softly by the glow of a small lamp. She waited for me to say something.

I said it. "I knew you wouldn't be up but I wanted to see you. Do you mind?"

"Certainly not. I'm flattered. Has anything happened?"

"Not anything—everything."

"Does that mean you've solved everything?"

"Not exactly," I said, "but almost. There's only one thing left and you can help me with that."

"Me?" If she was startled she hid it well. "But what can I do?"

"I'll tell you in a minute. First, I'd better bring you up to date. I found the money."

"Where was it?"

"In a locker at the airport—just where Cookie left it."

"How do you know for sure that Cookie left it there?"

"The key for one thing and a little information from a chap named Harley Perkins."

Her reaction was so slight that it almost escaped me. But there was a flicker of interest at the sound of his name.

"Do you know him?" I asked.

She nodded. "I believe I met him one night at Big Sam's. What information did he give you?"

"He told me that he drove Cookie to the airport and that Cookie had a suitcase. I found the suitcase, all right, but I also found an inquisitive cop." I patted my leg. "He gave me a souvenir."

"How awful!"

"The awful part came later. I went up to see Bertram and while I was in his apartment someone slugged Joe and grabbed the money. When I came down there was a reception committee waiting for me."

"But what did you do?"

"I didn't have any choice in the matter. They took me to Charlie Yee's and kept me prisoner while they sealed the money up in cans labelled 'Shrimp.' "

"Shrimp? Whatever for?"

"The money wasn't doing anyone much good in this country so Charlie was going to smuggle it out of the country."

"But where?"

"It didn't matter where. There are plenty of foreign governments that would be tickled to death to get their hands on a half a million dollars in U. S. currency. It's good anywhere in the world. In return they would give Charlie merchandise which he could import to this country and convert into spendable money. It was an ingenious scheme."

"What do you mean, 'was?' "

"I'm afraid I loused up their plans. I called Mac and tipped him off. He's probably raiding the joint right now."

"How were you able to do it if they were keeping you prisoner?"

I told her the story of my escape. Every detail. She listened with rapt interest. When I finished she didn't say a word.

"Not a very pretty story, is it?"

"You said there was more. What's the rest of it?"

"I'll tell you all about it if you fix me a drink."

She got up. "That's a fair exchange. Would you like it straight?"

"With soda, if it isn't too much trouble."

She fixed the drink and set it down on the coffee table in front of me. I reached for her arm but she was already moving back to her chair. "Why don't you sit here with me?" I said.

"I thought you'd be more comfortable by yourself. Besides, I want to hear the rest of it."

"Okay," I said, "suppose you recite your piece first."

Even in the poor light I could see the color draining from her face. "What do you mean?"

"When we were at dinner you told me that you had to find something out and that when you did you'd tell me about it. I'd like to hear it now."

"I'm afraid there is nothing I can tell you."

"I think there is. If you don't want to tell me, I'll tell you. But first I'll tell you the rest of it. The most perplexing part of this whole puzzle was Cookie's involvement. I knew Cookie fairly well, at least well enough to know that he wouldn't get mixed up in anything basically dishonest. So for the longest time I was trying to figure out just what his connection with the case was. I knew it couldn't be money so it had to be love."

"Love?" she said, "but Cookie—"

"Sure, I know, but they fall in love the same as other people. For a while Cookie and Harley Perkins were a hot item, then someone new came into the picture and Cookie promptly threw Harley over. Do you know who it was?"

She shook her head.

"It was Angel Face Lawrence. Do you remember the stranger sitting at the end of the bar in Big Sam's?"

"You mean that was Lawrence?"

"It had to be. After I left, to wait for you out back, Angel Face went to the pay phone in the rear of the building. There's a number you can dial to make your own phone ring. Telephone repair men use it to check out a phone. You dial the number and hang up. After you hang up the phone starts ringing and won't stop until you pick up the receiver. In this case, Big Sam picked up the receiver on the extension behind the bar. When he heard the phone stop ringing, Angel Face knew that Big Sam had answered so he picked up his receiver and asked for Cookie.

"When I questioned Big Sam about that call he told me that he didn't know who it was but that it sounded like one of Cookie's boy friends. Big Sam had Cookie answer the phone in the rear. In the meantime, Angel Face ducked into the men's room out of sight. You told me that the partitions of the rest rooms are thin and you could hear Cookie talking on the phone. So could Angel Face. That's how he knew just when Cookie was at the phone with his back turned. It was easy for him to sneak up on Cookie and put his hands around Cookie's neck."

She interrupted me. "You still haven't explained why Cookie was killed. If you said he wasn't involved because of the money, are you trying to say this was a crime of passion?"

I took a sip of my drink. "Hardly. Remember that Angel Face was wanted by the police. He was wanted desperately so he couldn't afford to expose himself too much in public. There were a lot of arrangements he had to have made so after he became intimately acquainted with Cookie, he could get Cookie to run a lot of errands for him."

"What sort of errands?"

"Oh, making arrangements for the trip to South America, for one thing."

"Angel Face wanted to be free to enjoy the money once the scheme was devised to cash in on it. He certainly didn't have too much freedom of movement here in San Francisco. I'm certain he was going to South America and it's reasonable to assume he was going to Argentina. We have no extradition agreement with Argentina so he would be safe there."

"How would he get the money through customs and what about a passport?"

"No problem. Bertram could get him a phony passport without too much trouble and Charlie could smuggle him his share of the loot after he and Bertram got their cut."

"You still haven't explained why Cookie was killed. Did he know too much?"

I took another sip of my drink. "He didn't know anything at first. He might never have known but I imagine he got curious. Angel Face probably fed Cookie some malarky about a business deal with Charlie Yee and asked Cookie to deliver the suitcase to Charlie. Among other feminine traits, Cookie had one that cost him his life—curiosity. He opened the suitcase and discovered the money. He must have known there was something fishy because nobody carries that much money around in a suitcase. Then he must have put two and two together and it came out Angel Face

Lawrence. He didn't know what to do. He was in love and he didn't want to expose his lover. I doubt that he realized the danger immediately so he probably thought he would talk things over with Angel Face. He took the money to the airport for safekeeping and then tried to contact Angel Face. When the money didn't arrive at Charlie Yee's I imagine there was all kinds of fur flying.

"This is all guesswork but I don't think I'm missing the mark too far. The word finally got back to Angel Face that the money didn't arrive so he contacted Cookie. Cookie must have told him that the money was safely stashed away in a locker and he had the key. Cookie then told Angel Face that he wanted to know where the money came from or something to that effect. Angel Face must have gotten nasty at this point and told Cookie to deliver the money or else. This is where I happened in on the scene."

"So Cookie was killed because he knew the identity of Lawrence?"

"Partially. He was killed, also, for the key. But before he was killed he deposited it in the pinball machine. After Angel Face killed him he started to drag the body out into the alley. But I was out there. He couldn't leave the body inside for fear of discovery so he had to slug me. After he slugged me he might have grabbed me under the armpits to lower me to the ground and in so doing discovered that I was wearing a shoulder holster. This gave him a perfect opportunity, he thought, to frame me for the murder."

"I'm afraid I can't buy that," she said. "According to the reports in the newspapers, no one was seen leaving the scene of the crime. If it happened as you described it, what happened to Lawrence? Did he disappear into thin air?"

"No, but he did the next best thing. He ducked back into Big Sam's and hid out in the men's room. He stayed there until long after the excitement had died down and then he forced the lock on the back door and beat it. Big Sam thought that someone had broken into the joint after he locked up for the night. It didn't occur to him that someone might want to break out instead."

"What about Peggy? Why was she killed?"

"Simple enough. Angel Face didn't find the key on Cookie so he must have surmised that Cookie gave it to someone else for safekeeping. He must have arrived at Peggy's apartment almost the same time I did. Then he saw me go in he had to wait until I left. As soon as I left, he killed Peggy and ransacked the place. When he still didn't find the key he thought Peggy must have given it to me. He must have called Bertram who called Charlie who sent Pinky over to my apartment to shake me down. You know the rest of it."

I picked up my drink and polished it off. I didn't like it. I said, "Do you want to tell me about your brother now?"

She jerked involuntarily. "What do you mean?"

"You know damn well what I mean. I think you've been honest with me right along. Whenever I asked you an embarrassing question, you didn't lie to me you merely sidestepped. When I asked you where he was, you didn't tell me, you merely said that the last letter you received from him was postmarked 'Nebraska.' It was probably no lie but at the same time it didn't answer my question."

"But what has all this to do with my brother?"

"It's just the other way around—what has your brother to do with all this? The answer is, your brother is Angel Face Lawrence."

She didn't say anything but her shoulders sagged.

"Your brother had you convinced of his innocence. He told you that if you'd hide him out it would give him an opportunity to establish his innocence. It must have been tough on him at first, being cooped up in this apartment, but he couldn't afford to leave. As long as he stayed here he was safe."

She said, "You used to be a cop. You know when the police look for someone they always check the relatives."

"Sure they do," I said, "when they can find them. But if you changed your name when you left Nebraska to come to California, how would they know who to look for? It was a perfect set-up for your brother but he might just as well have been in San Quentin because of the confinement here. He couldn't even step out for a haircut."

She looked at me sharply. "Then you know?"

"Of course I know. When his hair started growing long you realized what a striking resemblance there was between you. That's not odd considering you were brother and sister. Then he got the idea of dressing the part. With a little help from the Goodyear company, he could walk out of here dressed like you, with plenty of pancake make-up, and someone would have to know you real well and see you up close to tell you apart. Since he was already effeminate, he had no trouble acting the part.

"That was him I met on the street today after I'd been to the travel bureau. He made the dinner date and then came back here and told you to keep it. Otherwise, how would Pinky and Eddie know to wait for me outside Paoli's? That was him that Joe spotted near Harley Perkins' place. He must have gone to try to pump Harley for information but when he saw our headlights he got scared away.

"You wanted to tell me all this during dinner, remember? But you felt enough loyalty to your brother to confront him with the information I had given you and give him a chance to present his side of the story. But that was a mistake. A fatal mistake."

I got up and started walking toward the bedroom.

She arose hurriedly. "Where are you going?"

"To the bathroom. It's still in the same place, isn't it?"

"You can't go in there."

"Why not?"

"I—I don't want you to see the room, it's a mess."

"Yeah," I said. "I'll bet it is, Angel Face."

"What?"

"You can knock it off, you dirty bastard. I should have tumbled a long time ago. No wonder they call you 'Angel Face.' "

He squared his shoulders. "How did you know?"

"I would have caught on sooner or later. You helped me catch on sooner. Lorna knows I drink bourbon and soda. You served me Scotch." I nodded toward the bedroom. "She's in there, isn't she?"

He took a step toward me. "You dirty, lousy, no-good rat. You had to go sticking your nose in where it didn't belong. I had a perfect set-up and you had to spoil it. For two years I've been sweating this thing out and just when I'm ready to cash in, you come along. Two years," he screamed and took another step toward me. "Now you're going to get it. I killed those others because I had to. You—you're going to be different. This is going to be a pleasure."

"You can't get away with it."

He came closer.

I backed away. "The police will be here any minute."

He stopped. "You're bluffing."

"No, I'm not. Joe Pinsky was at police headquarters. He knows this is the only place I'd come."

"In that case, I'd better hurry." He jumped at me and had his hands around my throat before I could move. They were like a pair of steel vice grips. With two good hands I doubt if I could have broken his hold. I squirmed around but the grip only grew tighter. I grew dizzy and my lungs felt as though they were ready to burst. I tried to raise my feet and break the grip with the force of my weight. It was useless.

Then I did the only thing possible. It wouldn't have been as effective if he really was a woman. I brought my knee up between his legs. Hard. His grip loosened and I sucked in great big gobs of air. Then I gave it to him again. This time he doubled over. I caught a handful of that beautiful hair and jerked his head down as I brought my knee up. I heard a crunching sound as his nose gave way on my kneecap. I did it again for luck. As hard as I could, with a vengeance. His face was a pulpy mass of bloody flesh. He wasn't pretty anymore.

I let him fall to the floor. I watched him writhe around like a snake groaning with a horrible bubbly noise. Then I got sick. He wasn't groaning with pain, he was moaning with pleasure! The dirty son-of-a-bitch was not only a sexual pervert, he was a masochist! He got up on his hands and knees, rocking back and forth, trying to say something. I couldn't make it out but it sounded like, "More, more, more."

I heard the pounding of footsteps out in the corridor. I knew it had to be Mac. It was just a matter of seconds before the door would come flying open and—

There was less than a minute left to play and the score was tied. I had the ball and my only chance for a score was a field goal. I stepped back and took careful aim. When I swung my leg I put every ounce of energy into it. My toe caught him right under the chin and his head whipped back with a crack. He collapsed on the floor, dead. With a broken neck.

The front door burst open as I stepped into the bedroom. Lorna was lying across the bed, beautiful even in death. I knelt down at the side of the bed and stroked her hair. I kissed her cool forehead and whispered, "Good-bye, my darling."

www.ingramcontent.com/pod-product-compliance
Lightning Source LLC
Chambersburg PA
CBHW031230260626
47169CB00007B/2229